BINNY FOR SHORT

Binny

FOR SHORT

HILARY McKAY

with illustrations by
MICAH PLAYER

Margaret K. McElderry Books
New York * London * Toronto * Sydney * New Delhi

MARGARET K. McELDERRY BOOKS

An imprint of Simon & Schuster Children's Publishing Division

1230 Avenue of the Americas, New York, New York 10020

Published by arrangement with Hodder Children's Books,

a division of Hachette Children's Books

First published in Great Britain in 2013 by Hodder Children's Books

First U.S. edition, 2013

For information about special discounts for bulk purchases, please contact Simon &
Schuster Special Sales at 1-866-506-1949 or business@simonandschuster.com.

The Simon & Schuster Speakers Bureau can bring authors to your live event. For
more information or to book an event, contact the Simon & Schuster Speakers
Bureau at 1-866-248-3049 or visit our website at www.simonspeakers.com.

The text for this book is set in Bembo Std.

Manufactured in the United States of America

0613 FFG

2 4 6 8 10 9 7 5 3 1

Library of Congress Cataloging-in-Publication Data

McKay, Hilary.

Binny for short / Hilary McKay.—First U.S. edition.

pages   cm

Summary: Eleven-year-old Binny struggles to cope with her
father's death and the loss of her beloved dog while she adjusts to a
new home that might be haunted by her horrible Aunt Violet.

ISBN 978-1-4424-8275-3 (hardcover)—ISBN 978-1-4424-8277-7 (ebook)

[1. Family life—Fiction. 2. Loss (Psychology)—Fiction.

3. Moving, Household—Fiction.] I. Title.

PZ7.M4786574Bi 2013

[Fic]—dc23   2013000053

FIRST
EDITION

To Siân Grace Phillips, with many thanks for all the lovely letters and lots of love from Hilary McKay

(Alacrity is a wonderful word!)

List of Illustrations

BINNY FOR SHORT

The Rock Pools I

For Binny it had happened the way some people become friends. Totally. Inevitable from the beginning, like the shape of a shell.

Only it was not friends; it was enemies.

Binny had known at once that she was looking at her enemy, and the boy had known it too. The understanding was like a swift brightness between them.

It was not at all how Binny had planned things to be. Only the night before, Binny had worked out what to say to their silent new neighbor.

I know your name, *she would tell him, and then he would ask,* Yes, but what's yours?

Binny, Bin, Belinda, Bel. Mostly Binny. Call me Binny.

After that the first, hardest words would be safely over, and they would no longer be strangers. They would be Binny and Gareth. Easy, after that, to ask almost anything. Coming to the harbor? Do you think that ghosts are real? How far can you swim?

Anything.

After the first words.

That was Binny's idea, but it did not work out because she met Gareth at the wrong time, in the wrong place. She leaned out of her bedroom window and there he was, almost close enough to touch, leaning out of his.

Binny jumped with shock.

Pale sunlight caught the boy's glasses and flicked blank circles of scorn at her. His smile was not nice. He made a sneering, sniffing sound with his nose.

Binny abandoned all her earlier peaceful plans.

Battle, then. They would be enemies. They were enemies. No use to consider anything else. She had no problem with that. After all, she had not had a good, tough enemy for months. Not since the last one died.

All summer Binny and Gareth had been enemies. If things became dull, they had a very good way of spicing them up again. Two words. Irresistible. Dare you!

Binny and Gareth had dared and argued and squabbled their way through all the bright days of summer, until at last they had come to the final day.

This day, that had begun with the long trek to the headland, four miles farther down the coast.

Chapter One

By the time Binny was eleven years old, she had lived in two worlds. A child's world, and a time-to-start-growing-up-now world. An easy world, and a hard world.

Eight years in the first, and three in the second. Yet when Binny looked back at the first world from the second, it was hard to believe it had lasted so long. The eight years diminished like a landscape seen from far out at sea. An outline. Sunlit highlights. Some gull shrieks of dismay. A coldness, just as if a fog had rolled in from the sea. Then it was almost gone. A shadow land that once had been a solid, steady world.

That steady world had held Binny, her father and her mother, her brother, James, and her sister, Clem. It also held a large cheerful house, a friendly school, and her father's bookshop. Very famous people had visited that bookshop, and some of them wrote about it afterward. *The sort of bookshop you will find in Heaven,* wrote one optimistically. *Books to die for!* said another.

"That's an awful thing to say!" said Binny when she heard, but her family laughed at her, and her father had both quotations embossed on thick cream bookmarks, which he gave out free to customers. It was the sort of bookshop that gave away a lot of things free: bookmarks, sofas to sit on while you read, sweets in blue china bowls next to the sofas, iced water, stickers.

Even free stories.

The stories came from Binny's father. He had a large supply of them, which he shared with anyone who wanted to listen. Often that person was Binny. Binny seemed to have more need for stories than most people. Even when she was very young, she was a restless, bothered person. Stories allowed Binny to escape for a while.

"A long, long time ago," began her father one empty Sunday afternoon, when Binny was about six and in one of her fidgeting, no-one-to-play-with, climb-about moods, "in the days when there were heroes . . ."

"Aren't there still?" demanded Binny.

"Perhaps."

"Can girls be heroes?"

"As a matter of fact, girls usually make the best heroes of all . . . Are you going to listen, then? I can't tell stories to someone all tied up in a curtain."

"Why"

"They might miss something."

"What?"

"Something that matters."

"I can't hear you properly because I'm all swizzled up."

"Unswizzle, then. It might be important."

"It's only a story."

"Some stories are very important. Sometimes stories can save your life."

"Save your life?" asked Binny, unswizzling.

"I thought you'd hear that!"

"Tell me a story that could save my life! Go on! Start again! *A long, long time ago, in the days when there were heroes . . .*"

"What are you up to now?"

"Building a camp." Binny collected an armload of cushions, rolled the hearthrug into a log, and began digging a well with the TV remote. "Get on with the story!"

"In the days when there were heroes, which there still are, and nearly all girls too, there was a little house, in a little town, right on the edge of a wild, rocky coast. Right on the edge of the land this town was built, houses spilling down to the rocks. Salt spray blowing up the streets. Rock and stone and salt and wind and a sort of lightness in the air . . ."

(Here Binny crawled behind the sofa and began collecting firewood for her campfire by gently peeling away strips of wallpaper from the bottom of the wall.)

"And in that town," continued her father, in a rather louder voice, "there lived a girl whose name I forget."

"Call her Binny!" said Binny, popping out very suddenly.

"Lived a girl called Binny. In one of the little houses with hardly room to swing a cat, and the noise of her brother and sister, and the seagulls on the roof and chickens out the back, and the clatter of feet on the cobbles outside, and all the other sounds that there are in a place like that. So this girl, Binny, she used to go down to the sea to practice her singing..."

Soon, Binny-the-listener became Binny-from-the-story. The camp was transformed into a rocky shore. Seals sprawled like cushions in the shallows. The tide rose, and Binny climbed high amongst the rocks until she ended up perched upon a table, measuring the waves.

Binny was as good at listening to stories as her father was at telling them. His stories drifted around her head, and some stayed there and some vanished.

"Nothing vanishes," said Binny's mother, which turned out not to be true.

★ ★ ★

All this happened when Binny was very young indeed. In the first world, before it went forever. Before Max.

In that first world, for her eighth birthday, Binny had asked for a border collie puppy. "Black and white," she had ordered. "White socks, white stripe up his nose. White on the end of his tail. Look at the picture in my book!"

"No, no, no!" her mother had exclaimed, waving the picture away, but Binny's father had taken the book and looked.

Max the puppy, exactly like the picture in the book, had come rollicking into Binny's bedroom at dawn on the morning of her birthday. When Binny in the second world looked back to that far-off, lost world of her first eight years, it seemed incredible.

"It was," said Clem. "Ordinary eight-year-olds don't get border collie puppies for their birthdays."

It was incredible, but it was about to end. By the time Binny was nine, Max had gone. He had raced into Binny's life and out of it, all in a few months.

"Where? Where?" asked frantic Binny, but there seemed to be no answers. In the early days she was haunted by the fear that his unhappiness might be as bad as her own.

"Everyone's unhappy," said Clem, although not unkindly, and, "Try not to worry Mum."

Binny tried, but it was not easy. Remembering Max hurt. "It hurts my heart," she told Clem, hugging the cold ache in her stomach.

"That's not where your heart is," said Clem, sympathetic but accurate. "You'll get over it. You always get over things," added Clem, who didn't. "You'll get used to it and go on."

"I won't."

"You have to."

After Max, more than two years went by.

Binny was nine, then ten, then eleven.

By the time Binny reached eleven it seemed that Clem had been right. Half right at least. Max had gone and Binny, although she hadn't got over it, had got used to it. Just. Although for ages she had hoarded a box of dog biscuits in case Max should somehow find his way home, and even two years later she couldn't help gazing after any black and white dog she saw. She had survived, but she hadn't forgotten, and now it was a long time since she had last called "Max" and been flattened by his welcome. A long time since she had burrowed her face in his fur, or heard his terrifying roar at the sight of any stranger.

★　★　★

"But Clem was right, you have to go on," admitted Binny.

Going on was how the Cornwallis family—Clem, Binny, James, and Polly their mother—survived.

Chapter Two

Binny was pleased when she turned eleven.

"Grown up," she said.

"Not very grown up," said Clem, who was sixteen, cool, clever, and very grown up indeed.

Binny was green-eyed, with reddish-brown hair that hung in crinkled straggles: a seaweedy look.

"Oh well," she said, because six-year-old James's hair was spotlight gold while Clem's was silver gilt, smooth as pouring water.

"I don't care," she added, dragging her seaweed into two tatty bunches and tying them up by her ears. She really didn't care, even though sometimes it was hard work being sandwiched between Clem and James.

Clem was in her last year at school. Next she would go to sixth form college.

"If I pass my exams," she said cautiously.

"You know you will. Then what?" asked Binny.

"University, perhaps," said Clem, even more cautiously.

"To do music? With your flute?"

"If I can," murmured Clem. "If I can. If I can. If I can."

Binny did not doubt it. Clem seemed to have been born with a lucky gift for music, in the same way that some people had a gift for seeing ghosts, or turning cartwheels.

"Lucky!" protested Clem, when she heard this. "I practice and practice!"

"Yes, but even if you didn't you would still be able to do it."

"How?" demanded Clem scornfully.

"It's a sort of magic, I think," said Binny.

Binny herself had turned out to be very unmagical when it came to music. Her own plastic recorder (after a long time of Binny gnawing on the mouthpiece and hoping for a miracle) had become mildewed, loose at the joints, and warped into a curve from being cooked in the dishwasher. Finally, during the big clear-out, it had disappeared completely, along with many other items.

The big clear-out.

Bankruptcy.

The first dingy apartment, the first strange school.

"Why?" asked a nosy new neighbor.

"Because of Dad," said Binny.

"What did he do?"

"Died."

That was the calamity that had hit the Cornwallis family when Binny was eight. Their father had died.

Binny recovered the fastest, so quickly that a year or two later she could hardly remember being sad. I must have been, she thought guiltily. Very. Everyone was.

All the same, it seemed she got over the loss disgracefully quickly. Much faster than James, who for a time turned back to being a baby again. Faster than Clem too, who took ages to return to life. Even when the anniversaries came around—Father's Day, birthdays, the first Christmas—Binny had to think sad thoughts to make herself get the necessary tears in her eyes. The sad thoughts were not about her father either; she had almost forgotten how it had felt to have a father.

Clem guessed.

"How can you not remember him?" she asked.

"Of course I do," said Binny, and she hugged Clem and thought of how when her sister had played her flute, whatever her father was doing, however busy he was, he would listen, gently opening all the doors between the place where he was working and wherever Clem was practicing.

Poor Clem, thought Binny. Sometimes she also thought, poor James, remembering her father, infinitely patient, hour after hour, down on the floor with his creaking knees, laying out train tracks and miniature engines. There was no one now to play trains with James. The others tried, but they could not do it. James was too bossy and the boredom was too much for them. "Daddy! Daddy!" James had howled, beating the floor in rage.

Binny had never raged, nor huddled in misery. It made her feel bad. Perhaps, she thought, if I'd had a special thing, played a flute, or liked boring trains, it would have been the same for me.

But maybe not, because I still had Max.

While Binny had still had Max, it had been impossible to be wholly miserable.

Max did not understand that anyone had died. He was the only thing in the house that remained its identical, cheerful self. Max still emptied trash cans and gobbled up the contents. He still needed playing with. He still chewed the corners of rugs, dug holes in the garden, spun in circles of excitement at the sight of a ball, left puddles, yowled at strangers, and knocked over his friends. James had screeched to be rescued. Clem had pushed him away, but Max had made Binny laugh.

"Max was an awful dog," said James, years later, scrutinizing a blurry photo of Max attacking a cushion.

"You give me that and shut up!" ordered Binny.

James handed it over cheerfully, and turned to another picture, this time of his father.

"Very old," he said critically. "More like a granddad."

"He was twenty years older than Mum," said Binny, bending to look at the photograph. "She told me that when she married him all her friends and relations said 'Oh dear! Oh dear! Oh dear!'"

"He didn't pay the bills," remarked James. "Bills killed him."

"Clem says that's not true," said Binny.

Perhaps it wasn't, but all the same, after their father died, the bills were discovered. Everything went. The book-shop. The big house. The cars. The schools. The vacations. Binny's first world.

After the big house had come a very small apartment. It was in every way a horrible place, and no good at all for a large bouncy dog. At a family meeting it was decided that Max would have to live with Granny, who had a little house with a garden across the other side of town.

"I'll go as well, then," said Binny desperately. "Every weekend I'll go and live there! All the vacations too!"

"That would be far too much for Granny," said her mother, seeing the look of horror on Granny's face.

"I'm afraid it would," said Granny faintly.

"If you ask me," said Aunty Violet, in her cold, detached voice, "you are all being ridiculous. That dog should be properly re-homed."

"Properly re-homed!" repeated Binny, turning on her in amazement. "What do you mean, properly re-homed? And anyway, nobody *did* ask you!"

"And trained," said Aunty Violet, ignoring Binny completely. "Always presuming the creature is trainable, of course."

"Don't you call Max a creature!" exclaimed Binny. "Or I'll call YOU a creature!"

"Binny!" said her mother.

Binny marched out of the room, slamming the door behind her with a panel-splitting crack.

"Bang!" said James, with satisfaction, and crawled under the table, where he continued to repeat, "Bang!" over and over, turning it into a one-thought song, and rocking himself to the rhythm. Aunty Violet watched him without curiosity, murmuring, "I expect there's people he could see."

"What people? See about what?" asked Clem, but Granny said, "Clem dear, I should like a cup of tea," and Clem's moment of indignation passed. James continued to sing, Binny wept, with her arms around Max, and Aunty Violet went back to Spain, where she lived in a large rented apartment with no pets and no children. "Thank Heavens," said Aunty Violet.

Max lived with Granny for four or five months, so happy, rampageous, and noisy that every single one of her friends stopped visiting.

Aunty Violet flew back from Spain and did something about it, disappeared, and left Granny to do the explaining.

"He'll be far, far happier in his new place than with an old woman like me," said Granny when furiously confronted. "Anyway, it wasn't my decision, Binny darling. Aunty Violet thought it was best."

"I'd like to KILL Aunty Violet!" roared Binny.

For the next year or two, nothing went right. Binny and her family lived in one awful apartment after another, as their mother scurried from side to side across the country in search of the sort of job that would fit in with school hours, no car, three children, and no child care.

No word was ever heard of Max.

Sometimes, the children's mother thought she should try to trace him before it was too late. If only she had time, if only they lived in a place where Max would be possible, and if only there were not so many other problems.

Problems came like slapping waves, one after another, leaving the children's mother breathless. James was too young to notice, but Clem and Binny did, and they both got into the habit of protecting her as well as they could. For Binny this meant not making her feel worse by dragging the subject of Max into every possible conversation. For Clem it meant stubbornly organizing her own music lessons, which was much harder than it sounded.

"How much do they cost?" asked Binny. These bankrupt days she and Clem were very aware of how much things cost.

"Twenty-eight pounds an hour."

"Twenty-eight pounds an hour!"

"Dad used to pay."

"Couldn't you teach yourself?"

Clem shook her head. "You have to pass exams if you want to advance. Colleges want grades. I've looked it up. I can take the lessons at school and Mum will never need to worry."

"How can you pay for them?" asked Binny.

At first Clem managed.

"Do you mind," she asked her mother, "if I sell my skis? There's a notice on the notice board at school. Someone wanting them for this year's ski trip . . ."

There was no use pretending that Clem would be going on any more ski trips, so that was easy.

The skis paid for one term of lessons. Her bike for another. Clem said she didn't care. She didn't want bikes or skis; she didn't want anything except flute lessons, and she wouldn't have them if she couldn't pay for them herself.

Bit by bit, Clem's possessions began to disappear.

Ice skates. Camera. The collection of sparkling crystal animals.

"What, even the panda?" asked Binny, aghast.

Charm bracelet.

"It's only until I'm sixteen. Then I can get a job," said Clem.

The half of the bedroom that she shared with Binny became more and more empty. Binny watched in silence as books vanished to the secondhand bookshop, CDs to classmates. A beautiful red woolly jacket left its hanger in the wardrobe forever.

"Clem, that would have fit Binny next winter," said their mother.

"It had a label," said ruthless Clem.

Then came the dolls' house. One day Binny went into the bedroom to find Clem on her knees, and dolls' house furniture piled in a heap beside the painted rose that climbed the wooden walls. The dolls' house occupants: Calypso and Mr. Depp, Rosy Daisy and Timmy Green, the nameless baby who lived conveniently glued into a cradle, and their very large pet parrot, all cowered in silence on the roof. They were clearly in shock.

"Hi, Bin," said Clem, squirting polish.

It was Clem's dolls' house; it had never been Binny's, not even in an outgrown, passed on kind of way. At no time in Binny's life had she ever been interested in dolls.

Yet now she began to howl.

"Binny!" said Clem, astonished.

Howl, howl, howl, went Binny, pointing at the desolation.

"But you never ever looked at it!" exclaimed Clem.

"I know," sobbed Binny.

"Well, then? Oh, stop it, Bin! Stop it, Binny, *please*!"

"I know I didn't look at it," said Binny, sniffing and blubbering, "but I knew it was there. I didn't mind about the CDs you sold. It was okay about the books. There's books in the school library. I've got a jacket that will do this winter . . ."

"Oh, Binny!"

"But not Calypso and Mr. Depp and the parrot and everyone, Clem!"

★ ★ ★

The dolls' house stayed. Like a mutual reproach. Every time either Binny or Clem looked at it, they felt guilty. Nobody played with it ever again.

After a lot of desperate searching Clem found a paper round. Saturday mornings and Sunday mornings. Twelve pounds.

"Not enough," said Binny.

"No, it's not," said Clem. "I have to take out more papers than anyone else, yet we all get paid the same."

Clem was good at her paper round. She always closed gates, and she pushed the paper right through the letterbox, and she never made mistakes and left somebody out. "Good girl!" said the paper shop owner approvingly, but Clem did not want to be a good girl. She wanted fourteen pounds a week, and after a short fierce battle she got it.

"Wow!" said Binny. "That was brave!"

"It wasn't," said Clem. "I had to. If you want something badly, you have to fight."

Would I get Max back if I fought Aunty Violet? wondered Binny, nearly asleep in bed that night. Would it work?

It would be like fighting a stone, thought Binny.

Chapter Three

The last move of the Cornwallis family took them back to where they had started. The same town, but another apartment, a different school, and all the familiar places vaguely distorted, like reflections in water. People had also changed. Granny was in a nursing home. Soon after the return of the family she turned eighty, and forgot their names. A few weeks later, in the coldest part of the winter, she died.

"Pity it wasn't Aunty Violet," said Binny when she heard the news.

"You needn't have said that, Binny," said her mother.

It was nearly two years now since Aunty Violet had flown back from Spain to banish Max. Binny hadn't met her once in all that time, but she hadn't forgiven her either.

"Why can't I say it if it's true?" asked Binny. "Everyone knows Aunty Violet is a—"

"Binny, come with me for a minute!" said Clem, suddenly,

and she led the way into the bedroom they shared and shut the door.

"Say everything you want to say about Aunty Violet!" she commanded.

Binny said it.

Clem listened gravely, her eyes on Binny's unhappy, indignant, furious little face. "Is that it?" she asked, when Binny finally stopped.

Binny drew a deep breath and sighed.

Granny's funeral was arranged for a Saturday. The children's mother worried. A school day would have been easier. Saturday meant that either the whole family would have to go, or Binny and James would be left at home, with Clem in charge.

"I think all of us should go," said Clem.

"I think we should too," her mother agreed, "but there's James . . ."

"James will be fine, won't you, James?"

James sucked his fingers thoughtfully.

"And Binny . . ."

"I know."

". . . and Aunty Violet."

"What about Aunty Violet?" asked Binny, coming into

the kitchen to see what all the whispering was about, and she could not resist adding, "Horrible old witch woman!"

"Binny," said her mother. "Listen to me! Granny was Aunty Violet's sister. At the funeral she will be very sad. If you come with us on Saturday, I will be trusting you, *trusting you*, to be very polite."

"She gave away Max!"

"Yes, she did."

"Was that fair?"

"No, it wasn't."

"He could be dead."

"I don't think so. Can I trust you, Binny?"

"Oh, all right," growled Binny. "If Aunty Violet is polite on Saturday, I will be polite on Saturday."

Binny's family looked at her. James spoke the question that was in all their thoughts.

"What if Aunty Violet isn't polite on Saturday?"

There was a rather tense pause.

"If she isn't," said Binny at last, "I will still try to be. I mightn't be . . . but I'll try."

Saturday came, an icy day with a still gray sky that, just as they were starting out to the church, turned into tumbling white snow.

"Snow!" gloated James, zigzagging about the pavement with his mouth open, trying to catch snowflakes on his tongue. "Can't we have one little play in it?"

"Later. Not now. There isn't time."

"We could be late and say 'Oh sorry, we didn't know!'" suggested James, careering into a queue of people waiting for a bus.

"Be careful, James! Say sorry to those people! Grab him, Binny, and make him walk properly!"

Binny looped her scarf around her little brother and drove him like a Christmas reindeer. He pranced along, enchanted, with Binny skidding behind. They didn't look like they were going to a funeral.

"Can we go to the park after we've done Granny?" James demanded.

"I shouldn't think so," replied Binny, suddenly gloomy. "We won't be able to just rush off. We've got to be polite. I don't mind being polite to everyone else, but polite to *Aunty Violet*!"

James didn't care about Aunty Violet. He cared about snow, and he turned his question on Clem.

"Of course we won't be able to go to the park," said Clem. "We've got to go to a hotel for lunch."

"Why?"

"It's what you do," said Clem briefly. She had been quiet since she got up, unable to eat, overwhelmed by memories of her father's funeral. All the way to church, neither snow nor the need to be polite to Aunty Violet touched her at all. Once there, she sat as if in a dream, while on one side of her James fidgeted and on the other Binny sat rigid, enduring the presence of awful Aunty Violet.

Aunty Violet was not at all polite. She sat beside Binny's mother making rude remarks about the coldness of the church and the dismalness of the organ-playing. When the vicar got Granny's age wrong, she corrected him in a loud stern voice. At the end of the service she ordered Granny's friends to get off quickly to the hotel before they dropped dead from hypothermia, but she herself refused to leave the church until she had dragged the vicar around all the radiators to prove that only half of them were turned on.

Outside in the churchyard she was even worse.

"Friends' funerals I can just about tolerate!" she remarked to Binny's mother, gulping on the cigarette she had begun the moment they emerged. "Like-minded people there at the very least. But family funerals! Oh sorry, Polly! That was tactless of me!"

"Never mind," said the children's mother.

"Detest the damned things, though," continued Aunty

Violet loudly, "and there's no getting away from it. That was the second and they come in threes. You can't help looking around and wondering who's next! Whatever is the matter? *Whatever is the matter?*"

What was the matter was that Binny, after a whole morning of being polite, was suddenly creating a scene. Right there in the churchyard. Clenched fists, and stamping angry black footprints in the snow, exploding at Aunty Violet.

"What do you mean, saying things like that?" she shouted. "What do you mean, they come in threes? What do you mean, who's next?"

"Good Lord, I'm thankful I didn't have children!" said Aunty Violet, staring at Binny through a mist of blue smoke.

"I'm SICK of people dying! I'm SICK of funerals!" raged Binny, as if she had attended dozens, instead of only two. "I hate them and I hate you!"

"BINNY!" cried her mother, and grabbed and missed as Binny dodged.

Aunty Violet lit a second cigarette from her first, glanced at Binny with only a moderate amount of curiosity, and asked, "Is she the backward one, Polly, or was that the boy?"

"I know who should be next . . ." Binny yelled, and then was seized by her mother and muffled with a hug.

"I've gone dizzy," said Clem, very quietly, but nobody

heard because James, very annoyed at so much attention being directed toward Binny, suddenly began demanding, "IS there a toilet? IS there a toilet? Or shall I just go ANYWHERE?"

It began to snow again, one flake at a time and a million more waiting.

The last of Granny's friends, elderly people from her past, had all gone now, anxious to get out of the cold. Aunty Violet became busy with a largish hip flask. Binny's mother established a new grip on Binny. James joyfully began to prepare his next move.

"Polly!" snapped Aunty Violet, crossly. "For goodness sake, attend to that boy!"

Nobody noticed as Clem went whiter and whiter, drifted quietly across to an ancient Victorian table-shaped tomb, and passed out, cracking her head on the stone as she fell.

The snow became blinding.

"Wow!" cried James, going anywhere.

It was a minute or two before anyone noticed Clem, pale gold hair spread across the pale gray stone of the old tomb, snow white beneath the falling snow, very quiet and very cold.

Looking rather like she might be Aunty Violet's number three.

"Clem!" screamed Binny.

The vicar was very kind. By the time he discovered what was happening in his churchyard, Clem had begun to come round and show that she was alive, but he insisted on driving her to the hospital anyway. He took her mother too, and James who refused to be left behind. He would have squeezed in Binny as well, "although it would take some time to make the space," he admitted, having already shoveled a huge amount of junk from his backseat into his trunk to make room for Clem and James. "Perhaps she had better go on to the hotel with her aunt. I really think we ought to get Clem to the hospital as soon as we can. That bump is swelling quite quickly."

Which was how Aunty Violet and Binny ended up alone in Aunty Violet's cold and snowy car, having one last cigarette and waiting for the windshield to defrost enough for Aunty Violet to be able to drive.

While they waited, neither Aunty Violet nor Binny was polite.

First of all, Aunty Violet (puffing smoke like a dragon) gave her unflattering opinions on English weather, English funerals, the heating system in English hire cars, the terrible upbringing of English children, and, in particular, the shameful behavior of James.

After which Binny (glaring at the ashtray) made a few frightening remarks on the probable state of Aunty Violet's lungs, and then went on to add a great many more words about selfish disgusting old ladies who stole people's dogs.

This led to a listing of all poor Max's misdeeds as witnessed by Aunty Violet while visiting Granny. Smacking him, Aunty Violet added calmly, simply didn't bother him and had done no good at all.

"Smacking him?" screeched Binny. "Smacking him! You smacked him?"

"When I caught him chewing my purse, I certainly did!"

"I can't believe it! That's the worst thing I ever heard! I hope funerals do come in threes!"

"Oh, do you?"

"Yes, and I hope you're next!"

To Binny's rage, Aunty Violet burst out laughing, infuriating Binny so much that she pounded her seat with her fists. Clem had said that if you wanted anything badly enough you had to fight, and now she was fighting.

"I hate you!" she shouted. "I've hated you for years! I'll hate you forever! What did you do with Max?"

"Time we were on our way," said Aunty Violet.

"Tell me!"

"I wouldn't dream of telling you," said Aunty Violet

coldly. "Heaven knows how you would behave! He went to a very nice family. I met them only briefly—"

"Only briefly! *Only briefly!* How could you tell they were very nice if you met them only briefly? They might have been murderers! Where do they live?"

"This is ridiculous!" exclaimed Aunty Violet, lighting yet another cigarette. "First that squalid scene with your brother. Now this. Not to mention your sister. Does she often draw attention to herself like she did this morning?"

"Clem?" demanded Binny, so breathless at this accusation that for a moment she forgot about Max.

"Yes, Clem," said Aunty Violet, inhaling deeply.

"What do you mean? Because she fainted?"

"Mmmm."

"You make it sound like she did it on purpose!" said Binny, outraged.

"Didn't she?"

"Of course she didn't! Clem! She never would! Clem is the most private, most brave . . . You don't know her, so you'd never understand."

"Perhaps you're right."

"She was probably just cold. It's very cold."

"That's true."

Aunty Violet suddenly sounded less harsh. Almost as

if she really was sorry. It was the undoing of Binny: tears spilled down her cheeks. Aunty Violet offered tissues. Binny pushed them away and used her sleeves, the seat belt, and her funeral order of service.

"Binny. Listen to me."

"No!" said Binny, turned her face to the window, pulled up her hood, and stuck her fingers in her ears. "I won't listen. I can't bear you. You should be dead, not Granny. Dead. In a coffin. I wish you were. And I'd be glad."

"Would you?" said Aunty Violet quietly, and she nodded, and answered herself. "Yes."

Outside, the snow fell thicker than ever. Aunty Violet dropped her last cigarette from the window, sprayed on a vile flowery perfume, shook her hip flask, sighed, and started the engine. Then she and Binny skidded and slipped their way to the hotel, and neither of them spoke another word to the other, not that day, nor ever.

By nighttime Clem's memory of her grandmother's funeral was very vague, and mostly of the coldness of stone. James, in the blissful moment before sleep swept him away, recalled nothing more than the extreme pleasure of picking the right gravestone and going anywhere.

Binny, however, remembered every detail.

Do they come in threes? she wondered in the darkest

part of the night. Do they? Do they? Please God, she prayed, daylight pagan though she was, please God, no. Not Mum! Not Clem! Not James! Not even Aunty Violet, whatever I said in the car.

Praying did not work. Aunty Violet went back to Spain and almost immediately died.

"Binny'll be pleased," remarked James cheerfully.

Binny began a time of ice-cold, car-bound nightmares.

The Rock Pools II

It had been an odd day from the start, and not just because Binny had woken up in an apple tree. For one thing, it was the first time since she and Gareth had known each other that they had not been at war. It was not even a truce. It was an end, an unnaturally polite end that made the journey along the cliff paths like a journey with a stranger. Binny wondered if Gareth missed the warmth of battle as much as she missed it herself, but still, she kept up the peace. Many times she stopped herself complaining, "This was a stupid idea! We'll never get there!" Equally often Gareth had managed not to remark, "It would have been ten times faster if you hadn't lost my bike" Once he actually paused to hold aside a barbed spray of bramble so that Binny could pass. In return, when he stumbled, she asked, "Are you all right?" It was all very unnatural, and it seemed to make the way even longer. It was a great relief to climb the last rise and see the headland before them at last.

"Good! We've got it to ourselves!" said Gareth, hurrying to scramble down the steep slope that led to the rocky slabs beneath.

"I didn't want people around saying—Whoooahhh!" He slipped and skidded and landed on granite and forgot what he didn't want people around to say.

Binny arrived beside him a minute later, landing neatly between two rock pools. It was a rock pool landscape; a huge, almost level stretch of granite slabs, patterned in every crack and hollow with dozens of pools, each a small world of limpets, sea anemones, and transparent darting shadows.

"Little fish," said Binny, kneeling to look.

"Shrimps," corrected Gareth. "Hurry up!"

"There really is a fish," said Binny. "Look! Sitting on the bottom! Do you think he's ill?"

Gareth looked, admitted to the fish, identified it as a goby, not ill, just a natural bottom sitter, and relaxed into rock pool watching.

"What I like are hermit crabs," he said. "If you keep still you can sometimes see a shell, like that pointy white one, reach out legs—"

"Gareth, have you got your phone?" interrupted Binny

"Yes. Why?"

"Just that no one knows we're here."

"Well, that's good. They'd be after us if they did. Moaning. They like whelk shells, hermit crabs . . . anyway, come on!"

They had to cross a great bed of slippery black seaweed to reach the actual headland. Here enormous rocks, house-sized, car-sized, ankle-turning football-sized, were tumbled together with patches of shingle and pyramids of granite. There were very few rock pools now, just one or two, deep and cool, with shoals of tiny fish amongst their weeds. Gareth plunged an arm into the largest of them shoulder deep and pulled out a handful of spiky jellied unpleasantness.

"What's that" demanded Binny in disgust.

"Sea hare. Sea slugs, some people call them."

"Put it back! It's horrible."

"It's amazing," said Gareth, fishing out his phone to take a photograph. "It's the biggest I've ever seen. Where can I put it that's flat? Pull some seaweed, Bin, to make a background, and hold out your hands . . ."

"Me?" asked Binny, skipping hurriedly out of reach. "No thanks! Anyway, aren't you coming to look for the net?"

The net was the whole reason for them being there. A swathe of fishing net; a tangle of tough blue nylon. From land it was not visible, but earlier in the summer Binny and Gareth had spotted it from the little tourist boat that took holidaymakers out to see the seals. Gareth had seen the rubbish it had caught, plastic litter, stained sneakers, feathers, rags, and someone's diaper. Worst of all, a white gull, twisted and broken.

"How did it catch a bird?" Binny had wondered.

"Easy," Gareth had told her. "The gull would see something

moving just below the water, think it was fish, go in for a dive . . .
I suppose it drowned in the end."

Binny had shivered.

"Gareth!" Binny reminded him impatiently. "When are you going
to help? What about that net? Have you forgotten what we came
here for?"

"You just hardly ever see them," said Gareth defensively. "Sea
slugs, I mean. You can't just walk past!" All the same, he returned
his sea slug to its pool, resisted the temptation of a large green crab,
watching him from under a fan of seaweed with a look of insane
curiosity in its stalky eyes, and followed after the scornful Binny,
who could have walked past an ocean full of sea slugs without
a moment of regret. They slipped and scrambled until they were
far out on the headland, a place of rock and barnacle, neither sea
nor land.

"There!" exclaimed Binny suddenly. "I can see it!"

She ran, as well as anyone could run over a seaweedy bouldery
seabed, and Gareth hurried after her, dropped his glasses, moaned,
fumbled, trod on something that disintegrated with an ominous
crunch, and found them again. One lens left. The other a fractured
star, and where was Binny?

"Gareth! Gareth!" shouted Binny.

Chapter Four

Aunty Violet was dead, although not in Binny's nightmares. Nor did death decrease her powers to meddle in other people's affairs. Especially Binny's.

From beyond life Aunty Violet reached out and found her again.

A letter arrived.

"No. Please no," begged Binny.

(As if Aunty Violet ever listened to noes.)

Spain had been Aunty Violet's home for a very long time, but still, in England, she had owned a little house.

When she died, she left it to Binny and her family. That was what the letter from the lawyers said.

To Binny in particular. To Belinda Cornwallis. Also her mother, Polly Cornwallis, her sister, Clemency, and her brother, James.

They could sell it, and each have an equal share of the money it raised, or they could live in it as a family, whichever they chose.

I have been asked to state, remarked the lawyer who wrote the letter, *that this change to the will of Miss Violet Cornwallis was made after her recent conversation with her niece Belinda, to whom she sends her particular regards.*

"Her particular WHAT?" screeched Binny.

"Regards," said Clem. "It's like love . . . well, no, not love . . ."

Her voice trailed away as she spoke. The whole family was dazed.

"What did you say to her, Binny?" asked her mother. She had known the contents of the lawyer's letter before she read it aloud to the rest of the family, but still she was in shock. "*Whatever* did you say? Do you remember?"

Binny, who remembered too well every burning word, stared speechlessly at her mother.

"She must have liked you very much," said James, but his voice was full of disbelief.

"She couldn't have liked me very much," said Binny flatly.

Clem and her mother glanced at each other. Binny, even in the worst of her nightmares, had always refused to talk about the time she had spent with Aunty Violet while they were at the hospital.

"She's just done it to be nasty," said Binny.

"Binny, that's a silly thing to say."

"It isn't. If she wanted to be nice, she'd have told me what she did with Max. That's what I wanted. That's *all* I wanted. Not her horrible house! Or her rotten regards!"

"Did you talk about Max to Aunty Violet?" asked Clem curiously.

"I asked her where he was."

"Did she mind?"

"It was me who minded," said Binny. "He was my dog! She didn't care about anything!"

"She must have cared about something," said Clem. "She changed her will because of you. The rest of us are just tagged on. Even Mum."

"Even me," agreed James. "Me! And I'm the boy!"

Binny picked up James, turned him upside down, and lowered him gently into the trash can.

"Perhaps it was a good thing that you spent that afternoon together," suggested their mother, rescuing him. "It gave you a chance to get to know each other. I think she wanted to make friends with you. Maybe it would have happened, given time. Poor Aunty Violet. She couldn't have known she would die so soon."

Binny remembered the disgusting description she had given Aunty Violet of the probable black and oozing state of her smoker's lungs.

She could have known she would die, she said silently to herself, *I told her.*

"Her particular regards," said Clem, and she looked at Binny with thoughtful gray eyes.

"Oh, shut up!" snapped Binny.

"Regards," murmured James, nodding.

Binny flounced out of the room slamming the door, and flounced back in again a minute later with a large book. She read it with her back turned to everyone and her fingers in her ears, but it did not help much. The Aunty Violet discussion still went on. The opinion of Clem and her mother seemed to be that Aunty Violet's well-concealed heart of gold had been touched by her afternoon with Binny. Evidently Binny, as requested, had been polite. Lovable. Possibly even charming.

And so the house.

"I bet it stinks. I bet it's vile. She probably haunts it!" said Binny.

The solicitors sent photographs. It was a tiny house with an overgrown garden in a seaside town in the West Country. It was difficult to know what to do with it. Sell it? Rent it?

"Live in it," said James, not once, but a hundred times.

It was a house at the seaside. It was theirs. They should go and live in it immediately.

"We couldn't really," said Clem, but one evening when Binny was out of the way in the bathroom, she picked up the solicitors' photographs again. "It's miles away. And tiny. It would be like living in the dolls' house."

"I'd love to live in the dolls' house," said James, passionately.

"It's got a nice front door," said her mother, also dreaming over the photographs. "Those two steps up from the street . . . Actually, any front door that we didn't have to share with other people would be nice."

"We would have our own front door," said James, grabbing all the pictures for himself. "Our own two steps. Our own dolphin knocker. Our own basket thing with dead flowers in it. Our own . . . what's that supposed to be?"

"I think it's supposed to be a kitchen."

"Our own broken kitchen . . . our own . . . that's not a toilet, is it?"

"A very old-fashioned one."

"Our own . . . They've got that terrible TV program on in the apartment upstairs again!" James, who had been lying on his stomach, rolled onto his back, made his hands into a megaphone, and before anyone could stop him, bellowed, "TURN IT OFF! IT'S HORRIBLE!"

"James!" exclaimed his mother, and at the same time the sound of soupy dance music became much louder.

"If we lived in the seaside house," said James. "We'd have our own noise. And nobody else's."

The Cornwallises had got used to a lot of things since their first world vanished, but they had never quite got used to the tormenting noise of other people's lives. Footsteps on the stairs, the whine of local radio stations, and the thumping bass of forgotten music. Raised voices, slamming doors, midnight washing machines that sounded like jet planes, and an unseen baby that cried and cried. Worse still, their own noise tormented other people. James's roars, Binny's nightmares, and, most of all, Clem's flute caused a constant stream of complaints from the midnight washers, door slammers, invisible baby owners, and enjoyers of very loud radio and daytime TV.

"It would be lovely to have no one upstairs and no one downstairs," said Clem. "Our own house and nobody else's."

In all the years of worry and poverty and cramped homework in shared bedrooms, that was the closest she had ever come to complaining.

"We don't have to decide anything in a rush," said her mother. "Perhaps when the school year is over, we could go down. Maybe camp there for the summer while we think what to do . . . Hello, Binny! Nice bath?"

"You've got those pictures out again," said Binny. "You wouldn't really want to go and live in Aunty Violet's house?"

"Our house," corrected James.

"Yes, but not to live in."

"We have to do something with it," said Clem.

"Well then," burst out Binny, "it's easy! Sell it . . . wait, James, you haven't heard! Sell it, and buy back our old house!"

James began such a bellowing that Binny had to cover him with cushions and lie on top of him before she could continue.

"Think what we could do with all the money we would get! We could buy back our old house and the bookshop (you could work there, Mum!). Clem could have as many flute lessons as she liked. James could have another jungle gym. And we could pay for . . . (Keep still, James!) . . . pay for . . . (I'm not hurting you, so don't pretend I am) . . . pay for police detectives to track down Max!"

Clem groaned and her mother sighed. James's feet began a frantic drumming. Binny ignored them all and finished in triumph. "And everything would be exactly like it was before!"

The look that Clem gave her was freezing. Ice.

"Nearly exactly like it was before," admitted Binny. "Except for Dad. That's . . ."

Clem walked out of the room. Her mother followed.

". . . all," said Binny. "What's the matter with everyone? OUCH!" she added, as James escaped from his cushions so suddenly that her chin hit the floor.

"Nothing's the matter," said James. "Everyone is happy because we're going to live at the seaside."

"We're not!"

"We are!"

James retrieved the scattered cushions, arranged them into a nest shape, and flopped down on his back in the middle. He reached out a toe and switched on the television. Two worried-looking men were discussing the economy. James gazed at them with pleasure, sucking two fingers, wriggling deep into his cushions. He gave Binny a sideways glance to see if she was noticing how comfortable he was.

"The seaside," he murmured. "In our new house."

"It's not new, it's very, very old," said Binny. "It's old. It's broken. It's probably haunted. And it's mine more than anyone's and I'm not going to live in it. So there!" said Binny, and slammed out of the room.

Chapter Five

Binny wished she had never heard of Aunty Violet's house.

"No such place, no such old woman," she told Clem. "That's what I wish. Nowhere, never, and nothing to do with me."

It seemed to Binny that her family talked about nothing else. The thought of such a house, free, theirs, empty, and waiting, bewitched them all.

"I hate the idea," said Binny rebelliously, long after she had at last accepted that even if Aunty Violet's house could be sold for twenty times its real value, their old house and the bookshop, and all the way of life that had gone with those things, could never be bought back.

"Why do you hate it?" asked Clem, but Binny shook her head and would not explain.

"It's not because of school," said her mother privately to Clem. "She has to change school anyway this year."

Nor was it because Binny liked living in the troubled, grubby town.

"Why, then?" asked Clem, and answered herself, "Because it was Aunty Violet's."

Binny nodded.

"But not anymore, Bin."

"Don't you think we should sell it, Clem?"

Clem looked around the crowded, too-tight-to-fit apartment. She thought of their neighbor above, who detested them. Of the stairs in the dark. Of how often Binny had longed to push down the walls.

"No," said Clem.

It was James who finally ended the dilemma.

Whatever they did with the house in the end, arrangements had to be made for its care. One day the children's mother got up early and came home very late and paid a visit to the West Country in between.

"Without me," said James, when he discovered this treachery the next day, and he went and lay on his bed with his head in his arms. "I would have been good," he whispered, and then became alarmingly quiet.

His mother and sisters hovered over him.

"James, you would have hated it. All I did was talk to estate agents and chase spiders."

"I could have had some spiders for my farm."

"Binny and Clem were left behind too, you know."

"I've only got snails. Two snails."

"Two snails are plenty!" said Binny, who had been rather dismayed when James's farm expanded to include real, as well as plastic, livestock. "And you needn't be sad about being left behind yesterday. I was pleased I didn't have to go!"

"Did Mum tell you she was going, then?" asked James, his face still hidden in his pillow. "And did she tell Clem, too? Did everyone know except me?"

The silence that followed was so forlorn that they became reckless.

"Jump up, James, and put your shoes on, and we'll go to the park!"

"No, thank you, Mummy."

"Come on!" urged Clem. "I know what we'll do. We'll take your snails with us for a treat!"

James rolled over so that one eye became visible. He gazed thoughtfully at Clem.

"Do you think they'd like that?" he asked.

"They'd love it!" said Clem. "There's loads they could do there. Swings and the little train. Look!" She opened the ice cream box in which the snails lived and held it out to her brother. "They heard me talking and they've come out of their shells to listen! Look at their little faces! They're pleased!"

"Poor snails," said James, not looking.

"Can't disappoint them now that they're so excited!"

"Would you take them to the park without me, then, Clem?" asked James, and turned back to his pillow.

There was a long, unhappy silence.

James shrugged off hugs.

The snails withdrew.

The telephone rang and the children's mother left to answer it. Clem and Binny looked worriedly at each other. From the bed came a very small sniff.

"James, stop it," ordered Binny.

"I am trying to cry quietly," said James with dignity.

"I bet you're just pretending," said Binny, and rolled him over to check. James gazed up at her, hiccuping, reproachful, blotched with tears, and Binny gave in at last.

"All this fuss about not going to the seaside for one day, when soon we'll be there forever!"

"How will we?"

"If we go to live in Aunty Violet's house, like all of you want."

"But you said you wouldn't. 'It's mine more than anyone's,' you said, 'and I'm not going!'"

"Well, now I've changed my mind."

"Have you?" asked James, sitting up.

"Yes."

"Have you *really*?"

"Yes, I told you. Yes, yes, yes!"

James flung himself backward on his bed in a starfish shape. No trace of tears showed on his triumphant, shining face. He breathed like a person who had just won a great battle.

The end of term, which had felt like it would never arrive, now suddenly whooshed very much closer. Cardboard boxes began to appear in every room. In the three years since their father had died, the Cornwallis family had become very good at packing. Most of their possessions had dwindled to the bare necessities. The boxes, when filled, made a surprisingly small pile. Clem labeled them: *James, Binny, Clem. Kitchen, Nice Things, Books, Mum, Shoes*. Most of their furniture was going into storage until they found out exactly what was needed in Aunty Violet's house.

"I'm sure it won't be much," said Binny's mother. "There's quite a lot there already."

"What about beds?" asked Binny in horror.

"We'll take our own beds," said her mother, and Binny sighed with relief. Aunty Violet may have lived in Spain, she may have only visited her English house very rarely, but even so the thought of sleeping in any bed of hers made Binny's skin feel cold. She looked at her own bed with a new fondness after that, and even took to making it in the mornings.

Time rushed by.

"There is this night, then tomorrow night, then three more, and then it's THE DAY," announced James.

"I've never not looked forward to the vacations before," said Binny.

A van came and collected the beds and boxes. After that they camped at night on cushions and sofas, and ate from paper plates.

James's school term ended with a visit to a farm. He came home more determined to someday acquire his own vast acres.

Clem went to a prom with her hair piled on top of her head.

Binny's school held its Leavers' Prize Giving. Everyone had a prize for something. Between the more usual prizes for subjects like art and football were sandwiched such things as Fastest into the Lunch Line, Most Original Interpretation of School Uniform, and Class Chatterbox. Binny was astonished and delighted when Most Progress in Swimming was announced, and it was for her.

"Are you sure?" she asked, because although her swimming had progressed very much from the days when she sat on the side and absolutely refused to get into the water, it was, as it always had been, more wading than swimming. But they showed her her name on the prize certificate, *Binny Cornwallis*, curly letters and purple ink, and the applause when she went on stage was tremendous. Binny, who had thought since the day she began that she detested school, now found, in this last thirty minutes before leaving, that she loved it.

"It's not fair that I've got to go," she complained to her friends, but after all, everyone else her age was going too. They were all scattering. In September they would be starting again in new schools. They hugged each other and cried, but the moment they stepped out of the school gates for the last time, their tears magically dried. They looked over their shoulders, and school had already diminished, like a place viewed through the wrong end of a telescope.

Binny ran home through the park, and the air was entrancing. Cut grass and gas fumes and hot summer dust. The swing seats felt sticky. Three large girls approached, older than Binny, eyebrows plucked bare, and thick, sullen lips. They stood too close and chewed gum. "We're waiting," said one and Binny unpeeled from her swing and scampered away.

"Soon," she called, from a safe distance, "you'll still be here and I won't!"

Despite all her earlier protests about moving away, she found herself suddenly airy with excitement.

The day that they left passed like a series of pictures in a book. The seething sunlight of the city morning. The turmoil of the railway station. The shedding of the suburbs and spreading of the landscape into far horizons.

South and west rolled the train, sea on one side of the track, green fields on the other, bridges over wider and wider stretches of water, a station perched on a cliff top, a taxi that stopped at the foot of a lane so narrow that the driver could take them no farther. Then a climb along a twisting cobbled alley with cats at every corner, and they were there.

They knew what to expect because they had seen the photographs. The house had been forgotten and neglected for years. It was very small and beyond shabby, and furnished with a junk shop collection of bits and pieces. The children's mother had only been able to begin the cleaning it needed. All the spiders she had chased out seemed to have collected their friends and come back. It was probably haunted. The first thing Binny saw when she went into the sitting room was the reflection of a face that was not hers. *Bang, bang, bang,* went her heart as she stared at the rust-speckled mirror, and she couldn't help squeaking, "Clem!"

"What?"

"I saw something!"

"Please don't start, Bin!"

"That mirror. I saw her face."

Clem gave Binny a look, lifted the glass off the wall, and glanced in disgust at the cobwebs behind, so thick and dirty that they hung like rags.

"Can we throw that hideous mirror in the front room away?" she called to her mother upstairs.

"Throw anything you like away!" called her mother back cheerfully.

Clem marched outside with the mirror and came back a minute later empty-handed and said, "Gone."

"Thank you, Clem," said Binny gratefully, and then James screamed from somewhere above, "I can see the sea!" and Binny found herself racing upstairs, and sure enough, there beyond a lovely jumble of rooftops, and much closer than she had dreamed, was the patch of blue and silver.

"Our own sea," said James, with such deep contentment that Binny hugged him.

Their own house.

Their own front door. Nobody upstairs, and nobody down, and an enormous thickness of three-hundred-year-old stone between themselves and the houses on either side. Their beds were miraculously set up in the bedrooms. Within an hour they had discovered that from back door to beach took less than ninety seconds of racing through shortcuts and down flights of tumbling steps. Before the end of the afternoon Clem had walked into a café that said SATURDAY STAFF NEEDED, and been offered a kitten and given a job. By evening the children's mother had forced open all the windows, evicted the spiders once again, and shared out the bedrooms. They were all tiny, but still there was one each for Clem and Binny, a largish cupboard for James, and a sofa bed in the living room for their mother.

"One each for Binny and me?" asked Clem.

"Yes. You'll both need somewhere to do homework when school begins again. James can manage with just a little room for now, and I'll be perfectly happy downstairs. I can watch TV in bed, and have a real fire in winter. Stop worrying!"

Clem and Binny were still doubtful. Binny also had another problem.

"Which room was Aunty Violet's? Mine or Clem's or James's?"

"Well," said her mother cautiously. "Not James's, I don't think. Much too small."

"Mine or Clem's, then?"

"I suppose so."

Binny went back upstairs for another look at her room. It had a view over the rooftops and down to the cobbled street, and a trapdoor into the attic space.

"Nothing up there," said her mother, following Binny's gaze. "Empty. I checked."

"What if Aunty Violet suddenly popped out, though?" suggested James cheerfully. "All dead and going moldy! Binny wouldn't like that!"

"JAMES!"

"Well, she wouldn't."

"I think Binny and James should swap," said Clem. "James can live with the trapdoor and serve him right if a tiger pops out. Binny can have his room and she can come and do her homework with me if she hasn't space herself."

Binny looked thankfully at her sister. James stretched out on the floor beneath the trapdoor, longing for tigers.

"Can we swap?" Binny asked her mother.

"If that's what you'd like best."

"I would. I would," said Binny, and hurried to inspect

her new room, which was nothing but a box with a window and a miniature glimpse of sea.

"The kitchen," remarked Clem, peering over her shoulder, "is also absolutely dire!"

But Binny did not think her room was dire. It was too bare for that, and the kitchen, although truly dire, had a door that opened into a tangled garden. It was their own patch of outside, the first they had had for years. They loitered there for a long time that first evening, James on his stomach with the red and blue trains, Clem and her mother with cushions on the doorstep, Binny in the apple tree that grew by the fence.

"Stars!" remarked Clem, after a long dreaming time of not reading her book.

"Our own stars," said James.

Afterward, when Binny thought back to those first few days, she remembered two things.

The first was cleaning. Hard cleaning. Grime by the shovelful. A tremendous amount of scrubbing with water that began as rainbow-foamed buckets, and ended a thick, soupy black. The astonishing glitter of newly washed glass.

The second thing was freedom. A town as compact and bright as a rock pool two steps outside her front door.

Streets and little shops. Beaches, cliffs, a harbor, and a harbor wall. "Off you go if you want to explore," said her mother, finding her hovering on the doorstep that first morning.

"Can I really?"

"Watch out for traffic and don't fall in the harbor."

Binny, who had hardly ever been out alone, was uncertain at first. Down the street to stroke a cat. Back to the house very quickly, as if to check that it was still there. Find the baker's. Find the harbor. Then suddenly she was off.

And so were the rest of the family.

Before the end of that first week Clem had made a new friend, Binny had fallen speechlessly in love with the blond-haired boy who ran the seal trip boat for holidaymakers, and their mother had found a temporary job.

James had acquired a wetsuit from a beachside trash can. All by himself he had dragged it out, gloated over it, and smuggled it home.

It had a split seam down the back (One of them can mend that, thought James) and it contained an uncomfortable amount of sand in its folds. James shook the sand out on the bathroom floor, squeezed into it, swaggered down the stairs, and presented himself to his relations.

"James!" they all exclaimed.

It was lime green and candy pink.

"I love it, love it, love it!" said James. Never before had he worn anything like it, and he preened with pride at his reflection in the mirror.

"You can't wear that!" exclaimed Binny, absolutely scandalized. "Everyone'll think you're a girl!"

James became hilarious.

"Are you stupid, Bin?" he demanded, pointing magnificently to a very small wrinkle in the centre of the candy pink. "Have you ever seen a girl with *one of those!*"

To spare his feelings, Binny and Clem and Clem's new friend, Kate, from the café struggled through the front door before collapsing in the street.

"Girls," said James scornfully.

The days were so busy, so sandy, so filled with wind and sun, so different from any days that they had ever lived before, that at first for Binny, they swirled past in a dazzle of brightness. Only at night did the things she had lost come back from the shadows. "A long, long time ago," and the relentlessness of snow, and Max.

Chapter Six

The job that Clem had found so quickly was in a café by the harbor. Although it was owned by the aunt and uncle of Kate, her new friend, to the Cornwallis family it soon became simply "Kate's." Kate was older than Clem, and in school-time she was a student, but during the summer break she ran the café with such whirling, sparkling efficiency that her relations became background figures, hardly noticeable at all. It was Kate who chalked up the blackboard menus in twirly writing. Kate who had painted the gulls and the puffins that decorated the walls. Kate who watered the flower baskets, and picked the geranium flowers, a single stem for each table. She organized the photo gallery too: *Famous Faces We Have Fed*, all signed and some adding personal recommendations for their favorite café treats.

David and Victoria—Your Toasties Saved Our Lives!
Dr. Who—Best Coffee Outside the Tardis.

The Queen, Elizabeth R (in her actual crown)—Loved the Lemon Shortbread.

"Kate!" exclaimed Binny. "Where did she sit?" and she looked eagerly around the room, as if hoping to see the traces of scattered royal crumbs.

"Oh, Binny," said Kate, and grinned.

Kate and Clem were friends from the start, and Clem's Saturday job soon expanded to include extra hours for busy times. Kate renewed her offer of a kitten, and Clem came home one evening and said, "There's two little spotty ones, and another, snow white . . ."

Binny looked up, suddenly annoyed.

"Like a handful of cloud," said Clem.

It was so easy for Clem. A kitten. No problem. The only difficulty to pick the color.

"I'd rather have a dog," said Binny. "Max."

"I'd rather have proper farm animals," said James, sucking jam off his toast and getting blobs of it on his chin. "A horse, some cows, some sheep with black legs and black faces, a pig mother with babies, those things that aren't camels . . ."

"Llamas," supplied Clem.

"Llamas, two donkeys, chickens, ducks . . ."

"We could manage a kitten," said the children's mother thoughtfully.

"Max!" repeated Binny. "Why doesn't anyone take any notice of me? This is practically my house, in case you'd forgotten. None of you would be here if it wasn't for me!"

"Binny! The handle's come off your toilet again!"

"I've given you back all the spiders you had in my room, Bin. I've put them under your bed."

"Look, Binny!" said James, sneezing as he upended an ancient box from a cupboard. "Loads and loads of old lady underwear!"

"All yours, Binny!" said Clem cheerfully. "Waiting for you to grow into them."

A reluctant sort of giggle began to develop deep in Binny's stomach.

"Your bath wobbles, Binny," remarked her mother. "And I'm afraid your electricity bill was your only mail."

"Binny," said Clem. "Under your sink in your kitchen you've got a very old mousetrap, and I'm really, really sorry to say you've caught a very old mouse . . ."

"STOP IT!" yelled Binny.

Later she went with Clem to look at the kittens. Their blundering littleness reminded her of Max. It was impossible not to choose the white one.

"When you've got it," said Binny to Clem as they walked back up the hill together, "don't ever let anyone take it away."

Clem gave her a quick, kind hug.

"Help me choose a name," she said.

Snowball, Mittens, Candyfloss. Mist, Daisy, Crystal.

Clem was happy, thought Binny. There was the kitten. There was her job, which in turn was flute lessons, independence, and the cheerful company of Kate. Also with Kate came the added bonus of Liam, her older brother. It was Liam who ran the seal trips in his granddad's old boat, immodestly renamed by its new owner *The GoGettaGirl*.

"Liam, Liam," wrote Binny, in loopy letters in the wet sand at the edge of the sea. He was so beautiful that she went down to the harbor at least once a day, just to look at him.

He didn't know she existed.

James also wrote on the sand.

James

in fat contented letters. He too was happy. He had got his own way. There they were, at the seaside. Two or three times a day he would drag someone down to the beach, just to check it was still there. He loved it all: the overgrown strip of garden, the speechless silken nights when there was not a single person with the energy to force him to bed, his room with the high window and the dead flower basket directly underneath. If he stood on a chair and leaned perilously out, he could reach that basket. Late in the evenings he liked to do that, dropping the dry gray flowers one by one into the street below. Then the basket was empty.

James stirred it with a stick and thought.

Very soon afterward, the basket turned green.

"Lettuce!" James told Binny proudly when she noticed. "Like we grew at school."

"Where did you get the seeds?"

"At the supermarket, with Mum," said James. "Buy One Get One Free." He did not add that he had taken this order to be a two-part command. Buy one! Get one free! James had obeyed the second part, but postponed the first. He did not think anyone needed to know that while he had waited idly by the flower seed stand, sucking the two fingers on his left hand that he always sucked, and smiling dreamily at the checkout lines, his right hand, almost without him noticing, had gently removed the lettuce seeds from their place in the rack, and allowed them to drift into his pocket.

Now they were growing. Wonderful. The seaside, the garden, his lettuce seeds, his duffel bag full of plastic farm animals from the charity shop, his glorious pink and lime green wetsuit.

Often James lay in bed at night and counted his blessings.

Somehow, Binny remained a little outside all this happiness. The others had no guilty consciences to haunt them; they had fought no icy bitter battles, they had willed no vengeful deaths. No voices echoed in their minds; *Binny. Listen to me.* No enemy had sent to them *particular regards.*

Binny had found out what that meant now.

"Regards?" Kate had asked. "Well, if someone regards something, they look at it. Hard. Carefully. I suppose you might say..."—she glanced around the café for an example—"'See how that woman by the window regards the menu!'"

The woman at the café window was scrutinizing the menu as if she was deciding between two alternatives. *Shall I be cheated? Or shall I be poisoned?* Binny looked at her cold, unfriendly face, and her skin prickled at the thought of Aunty Violet's particular regards. The regards were the worst thing. Worse than all the other manifestations of Aunty Violet's haunting: the nighttime sound of a heavy step on the stair, the sudden glimpses of a familiar figure in a street of strangers, the pale stern reflections that no one else noticed.

"Or," continued Kate, still thinking of Binny's original

question, "you can send someone your regards . . . like a
message—"

"I don't want to know any more, thank you, Kate," interrupted Binny.

"Oh . . ."

"If you don't mind."

"Are you a bit down, Bin?"

"No. Yes. No," said Binny.

The view from the café window was like a picture in
a book. The busy street and the bright harbor. The pencil
blue arc of horizon between sea and sky. The white gulls,
bold as pirates, raiding picnics. People flapped them away
and they screamed back, amused and loud and jeering, as
they spiraled up invisible staircases of air. Their wingbeats
lifted the shadows.

"I think I'll go out," Binny told Kate. "I'll go down to the
harbor. I'll just tell them at home."

At home her mother and Clem were clearing cupboards
into garbage bags. James was unhelpfully supervising, and at
the same time hunting spiders for his farm.

"Take him with you!" begged Clem, when Binny arrived.

"Oh, all right," agreed Binny, "if he wants."

James was always happy to go to the harbor. He collected his crab line and a handful of salami for bait and

trotted after Binny down the sunlit street. She planted him by some lobster pots and went to gaze at Liam. *Speak to me!* she willed him silently.

Liam didn't. He never did, no matter how hard Binny squeezed her hands and hoped. He just carried on counting his takings from the last boat trip.

"Hi," said Binny, bravely.

Liam briefly half raised one eyebrow.

"I know who you are!"

"Yeah?"

"You're Kate's brother."

"Um."

"Kate's my sister Clem's friend. Her new friend. They work together."

"Right." Liam pushed his money in his pocket and vaulted out of his boat onto the harbor steps.

"That's my brother!" Binny nodded toward James, who was already fishing over the wall, sharing the bait with the crabs, sometimes a nibble for them, sometimes a nibble for himself.

Liam glanced briefly at James in his wetsuit and asked, "Sure he's not a girl?"

"Yes. Definitely. He's not. Don't ask him. We didn't buy him that wetsuit. He just found it in a trash can."

"Ah."

Was that a question? wondered Binny. To embark upon the history of the wetsuit or not? Yes? No?

No. Liam was turning away.

"I wish I could come on your boat," she said all in a rush.

Liam paused, and then said, suddenly amiable, "Plenty of room."

Binny lit up.

"I'll be back in a minute. Four pounds fifty."

"Four pounds fifty!" repeated Binny, absolutely staggered. "Four pounds fifty? Even though I know Kate?"

"Everyone knows Kate," said Liam, sauntering off.

Binny sighed and looked down at her feet, and a miracle happened.

A scrap of paper.

A five-pound note.

It blew past Binny's grubby sneakers and plastered itself against the lobster pots. Binny flung herself after, and seized it. A few minutes later, when Liam returned, she rushed to him beaming.

"Look what I found after you'd gone!" she said, holding it out triumphantly.

"Thanks," Liam said, calmly pocketing it. "Not often I drop a five-pound note."

Binny gave such a squeak of indignation that for once he actually looked at her. Then he grinned.

"Go on, then! Hop in!"

"Now?"

"Yep."

For a moment Binny hesitated. There was James, age six, hanging over the edge of the harbor wall. Still, James's sense of self-preservation was very acute. He probably wouldn't fall in and even if he did, the harbor was swarming with people who would rescue him. People in wetsuits. People with boats. Someone would fish him out.

"How long does it take?" she asked, turning back to Liam.

"Depends where the seals are. Are you coming or not?"

"Coming," said Binny.

Liam's seal trip rides had one purpose. To see seals. Once the seals were seen, cooed over, and photographed by his passengers, he headed back to harbor by the shortest route. If the seals were close, on the rocks at the other side of the bay, then people had a very fast trip. If the seals were not there, he begrudgingly took his boat farther. His aim was to pack in as many journeys each day as daylight would allow. Nothing, not diving gannets, porpoises, seasick passengers, overboard hats, seascapes, or landscapes, could persuade him to pause or turn out of his way. Once a basking shark had stopped him in his tracks. Once. Such had been the outcry on the boat when the passengers realized that Liam intended to just hurry past.

This was because Liam was not only stunningly good-looking (golden skin, bleached brown hair), and superbly agile (he swung and balanced with catlike grace amongst the benches and life jackets and clutter-burdened holiday-makers that filled his little boat) but also quite amazingly economical.

On Binny's first trip they found the seals just across the bay, and so Binny was back before James even noticed she was gone.

"Thank you! Thank you!" she said to Liam (now posing for photographs beside a large money box labeled *Comforts for the Crew*). "Hullo, James!"

James did not look up. He had five crabs in his yellow plastic bucket and he was busy detaching a sixth from his line. It was a little green one, and its beady eyes glared at James as he removed the last piece of salami from its jaws and ate it, all dripping with harbor water.

"Gravy," Binny heard him murmur, and then he noticed her and said, "Look!"

"Lovely," said Binny, peering into the bucket.

"You can't see them properly like that," said James, and

began lifting out his victims one by one and arranging them in a fidgety row.

"Mum," he said, touching the first with a grubby finger, "Daddy. Clem. You. Me, that's the best one. And the one I've just caught."

"That can be Max."

"No. That's Clem's kitten when she gets it."

"You can't have Dad and Clem's kitten at the same time."

"Why?" asked James, repacking his bucket.

"Because Clem's kitten and Dad were never alive at the same time."

"In my bucket they are," said James.

"Well, then, your bucket's not real life!" complained Binny.

James tied the bucket handle to his crab line and gently lowered it into the water. "They're going back to their homes now," he said, and jiggled the line until the crabs were all gone. "You can't say the harbor's not real life."

"James, do you remember him?" Binny asked suddenly.

"Who?"

"Dad."

"'Course I do," said James cheerfully. "He's not as dead as all that!"

Chapter Seven

The children's mother was good at finding jobs, and she found one almost at once.

"Just a few hours a day," she said. "Temporary, because they're short of staff in the vacation season."

"But aren't you going to have a vacation too?" protested Binny.

"A working vacation," said her mother. "I think it's wonderful. It will make all the difference. I can even take James if I need to. But what will you and Clem do with yourselves all day?"

"I'm going to paint the kitchen," said Clem. "I can't bear one more day of that awful color. Who ever would paint a kitchen pink? And the marks on the ceiling make it look like someone's been murdered in the room above. And no, you can't help, Binny, so don't ask!"

Clem enjoyed painting. She had done it before. But she liked to work alone. She did not welcome the company of other people, kicking over paint cans and demanding to know what they could do next.

"Can I choose the color?" asked Binny.

"Nope. You'll choose yellow."

"I think yellow would be just right."

"You always do. And it never is."

"Oh well," said Binny, "I'm definitely painting my bedroom yellow. When I can be bothered. If you're doing the kitchen, I'll clear up the garden. That's the next worst thing. And when I've finished, I'm going to build a tree house in the apple tree."

"Wonderful," said her mother. "There's a spade in a corner if you want to dig. It's a bit rusty, but it will still work. I expect James will help you, won't you, James?"

"If I have time," said James.

"We might find anything," Binny said, prowling around the garden for a good place to start. "Treasure or anything. There could be all sorts buried, for all we know!"

She began very optimistically straight after breakfast the next day, but the morning passed with no hint of treasure. After hours of dragging up armloads of rubbish, Binny had found nothing but brambles, nettles, a handful of green and ancient seashells, and a hot-looking, leathery toad.

"Give him to me," said James, who had set up his farm

and was greedy for livestock, but the toad burrowed into a forest of nettles before he could be given to anyone.

"There's plenty of earwigs, if you'd like them instead," offered Binny.

"I'd rather have the toad. Why did you let him go?"

"I didn't. He just went."

"He could have been a cow for me," said James regretfully. "I could have had toad milk."

"Yuk!"

"Not yuk. Lovely. Lovely, lovely toad milk."

"Shut up and come and hold this bag while I fill it. You're not helping at all."

"When are you going to build the tree house?"

"Soon," said Binny, and she stopped work to look affectionately up at the apple tree. It was the largest she had ever seen, its branches spreading in huge sweeps over the garden, weighed down with green apples and clouded with leaves.

"I think it looks friendly," she said to James.

"Friendly?"

"Don't you love it?"

"No," said James and after a time added, "because."

"Because what?"

"Because it's a *tree*," said James.

★ ★ ★

Late in the afternoon, deep amongst the waist-high grasses,
Binny found an old red rubber ring, a dog toy, tooth-marked
all over and faded to pink.

"Max had one like that," she said, holding it up for James
to see.

James, who was lying on his stomach annoying ants, did
not even glance at it.

"James, *look* what I've found! Doesn't it remind you?"

"Bin's getting in a state," James remarked to the ants.

"I'm not!"

"One of her states."

"I was just remembering," said Binny, and she held the
faded rubber ring to her cheek, as if it was something
precious, instead of one of a million of its kind, made for
one of a million dogs.

"Max was too big," said James.

"He was not!"

"He was bigger than me and he knocked me down."

"That was only playing!"

"And he chewed my arms and legs. I remember."

"No, you don't! Not properly. You couldn't, you were
just a rubbish little toddler! About two or something."

"I was older'n that," said James with dignity. "And I

remember a lot. You couldn't open the front door when anyone came to the house in case he killed the people on the other side. That wasn't very good. And he stole things. Birthday cakes."

"Once!" said Binny. "Once *only* he stole *one* birthday cake . . ."

"Mine," James told the ants. "That boy is listening to everything we say."

"What boy?" asked Binny, looking round, startled.

"Staring and listening, there at the window," said James, and pointed at the house next door to theirs.

"There isn't a boy," said Binny. "That house is empty. Stop trying to change the subject!"

"What subject?"

"James!!!" wailed Binny, but it was no use wailing at James because as far as anyone could tell, he lived like a boy in a bubble, entirely in his own world. Completely useless when a bit of sympathy was required. Binny, still holding the rubber ring, went to find Clem.

Clem was enjoying herself and not wanting anyone.

"Go away!" she ordered the moment Binny appeared in the kitchen. "Don't go near anything! It's all wet paint! *Look* what you've done! I knew you would!"

"Clem, I found this."

Clem glanced across at the rubber ring—which was clearly a dog's toy—and said, "Oh?"

"Don't act like you've forgotten Max."

"I wasn't," said Clem, as she brushed fresh paint over Binny's smudges. "I remember Max. I remember Dad. I remember Granny. I remember Aunty..."

Binny did not want to remember anyone but Max, and so she left Clem and went and sat on the doorstep until her mother came climbing up the narrow street, her hands full of bags.

"Binny, Bin, Bel, Belinda!" she exclaimed, dropping down on the step beside Binny. "Poor old Bin! You've got paint in your hair."

"I know." Binny leaned thankfully against her mother and it was like leaning against a thin, springy tree.

"What have you been up to, then?"

"Nothing."

Her mother laughed.

"Well, Clem's been painting the kitchen. And I started clearing up in the garden. I filled the whole trash can and five garbage bags."

"Oh, well done, Binny! Have you been working all day?"

"Not all of it. Earlier we went down to the beach. I found a washed-up surfboard broken in half. I've brought it back.

I thought I could make it into a small one for James but Clem says he'll drown."

"Don't let's drown James," said her mother. "You never know, sometime he might come in useful."

"He's been wearing that awful wetsuit all day. Even into town. Couldn't we take it off him and buy him a proper one? He was terrible in the paint shop when they thought he was a girl."

"He's only six," said Binny's mother, an excuse that in Binny's opinion was made far too often for her little brother.

"When I was six, did I take my clothes off in shops?" she demanded.

"Well. No. Anyway, tomorrow you won't have to worry about him. I'm taking him into work with me. He loved it when I took him before. Being spoiled."

The work that Binny's mother had found was in an old people's home. She had been jubilant to discover a job within walking distance of home, and no amount of cunning questioning by Binny could make her admit that she did not enjoy it. She was brave, and she had a way of making other people feel brave as well.

"Breathe that air!" she told the old ladies she worked with, opening windows and letting in weather. She made them laugh, and so did James, gobbling the cookies they fed him and hanging over the chickens that lived in the garden.

Still Binny worried.

"You look tired."

"Not at all."

"And you smell like hospitals."

"That's just the soap we use."

"Promise it's not awful."

"I promise it's not awful. It's . . . it's . . ."

"What?"

"Kind," said her mother, who always found, if she could, the right word.

Binny's mood suddenly lifted, like a balloon let go into the wind. She jumped up from the doorstep just as the door opened behind her.

James appeared.

"Hello, don't kiss me!" he said, his invariable greeting whenever he met a member of his family. "Wait till you see what Clem's done in the kitchen! Come on!"

"Grab him!" screeched Clem, from the depths of the house. "It's taken ages and it's still wet. Watch Binny too!"

"I'm being careful," Binny told her. "Clem! Wow!"

Since her last visit, all the painting clutter had been cleared from the kitchen. The window was sparkling, the floor scrubbed.

"That greeny-blue is wonderful," said Binny. "And I thought it would be awful when I saw it in the shop!"

"Clem, you're a genius," said her mother, appearing at the door with James. "It's transformed!"

"I'm painting the cupboard doors tomorrow," said Clem, turning away and washing her brushes with extra care so as to hide her pleasure at their praise. "White. Goldy-orange round the edges of the panels."

"This room has doubled in size!" said their mother, looking around. "How did you do that?"

"Put the cooker in the garden!" shouted James.

"Good heavens!"

"All of us! Carrying! Even down the steps!"

"The cable just reaches through the window," said Clem. "We can cook out there tonight while the paint dries."

"Then that boy will stare," said James. "With his glasses."

There really were new people next door. The house, which was twice the size of theirs, had been opened up that afternoon. Because of the thickness of the walls they heard nothing when they were indoors, but in the garden they caught voices, a man and a woman.

"Posh voices," said Binny.

They did not hear the boy, but they heard his name called: Gareth, several times, impatiently. And then the house next door became quiet and they forgot their new neighbors in the magic of the evening. Cooking flatbread in the garden, chopping tomatoes, lighting pale candles, dreaming amongst the brambles and nettles.

"I'm going to look at the harbor," said Clem, restless because the sky was turning to the purples and indigos of night. She vanished almost at once, before Binny could begin to say, "Wait for me!"

"Can I run after her?" she asked.

"Sorry, but it's too late for you, Binny. And she'll be meeting her friends. Kate and her brother. Leave the candles alone, James."

"Seen all my weeding?" asked James.

"Yes, fantastic. You must have worked so hard."

"Binny helped," said James kindly. "She—"

"James, I saw that!" interrupted Binny suddenly.

James stopped speaking and glared, fists clenched behind his back.

"He's got the matches," said Binny, so James was swooped up, frisked, and carted away. He was so much smaller than the rest of his family, so light-boned and portable, that he was very often swept up and deposited in a more convenient place.

"Bed!" said his mother.

"Will you read me a story?"

"When have I ever not read you a story?"

Now Binny was alone in the garden, and it was no longer magical, but eerie. Outside the circle of candlelight the world was all shadows. The windows of the house next door were like black empty eyes. Something rustled; it might have been the toad.

"Time to come in?" asked her mother, reappearing in the doorway.

"Yes," said Binny.

The Rock Pools III

Binny looked like a victim of the fishing net herself. Alarmed, bedraggled, struggling to stay upright as she staggered under its weight.

"It's much bigger than I thought it was!" she gasped to Gareth as he reached her. "And it's full of stones and I can't tip them out."

Gareth came and added his strength to hers, but it did not make much difference. At least half of the net was under the water, and it was laden with shingle piled up by the sea. Also it was right at the edge of the breaking waves. As fast as they managed to tug a section free, the sea caught it and dragged it out of their hands.

"This will take forever," said Gareth. "You stay here and keep hold of the net. Gather it up as it gets loose. I'll wade in and lift out the stones one by one. Once we get the big ones away, it will be easier."

This plan worked and the net lifted free, just as a sudden wave enveloped them both in an explosion of spray. For a few seconds they lost sight of each other, reeling about like ghosts in a snowstorm.

"Get back to the rocks!" shouted Gareth. "Hurry!"

Binny was only too glad to do that. She hoisted up the wet netting, all tangled with rubbish and seaweed and feathers, and turned to run. As she did so, her fingers gripped something unseen.

Something clammy that smelled dreadful, and disintegrated into slime and bones. It was too much for Binny; she shrieked and flung away her armload of net. Gareth dived and rescued it just before it was swept out to sea.

It was a struggle to reach the higher ground; Gareth half-blind, and breathing in gasps, Binny wailing, "What was it? What was it?"

"Dog fish," said Gareth.

"I thought it was a dead baby seal!"

"Gone now. Washed out," said Gareth.

His voice sounded so odd that Binny was startled. For the first time she looked at him properly.

"What's the matter?"

His face was gray and waxy with sweat and he was half crouched over his armload of net.

"My arm."

Taut, from the top of Gareth's right arm to the tangle of net across his knees, ran an inverted V shape of black line. Blood oozed from the point of the V. The dark shaft of a buried fish hook stuck out from the muscle.

"Oh, Gareth," said Binny.

"Don't just say, 'Oh Gareth!'"

"What is it?"

"It's a mackerel hook. There's a whole line of them tangled up in this net. Great rotten rusty things with barbs on to stop them coming out!"

"You'll have to go to the doctor's," said Binny, wisely. "Have a jab, probably . . ."

"How'm I going to get to a doctor's?" demanded Gareth. "How'm I going to get anywhere with this stuck in my arm and the rest of the line all lost in the net?"

"Can't you just pull?"

"No, I can't!"

"If we had a knife, we could cut the line. Then could you manage?"

"We haven't a knife."

"Or anything sharp!"

"Like what?"

Binny thought of shells, and left Gareth while she found one.

With it she sawed away at the line while he flinched and complained. The edge of the shell wore away, but the line remained uncut.

"You'll have to pull it," said Binny at last.

"I can't."

"One pull. Just pull."

Left-handed, Gareth reached for the shaft of the mackerel hook, pulled, and clung to the rock as if it had suddenly swayed.

"You do it!"

Binny quailed.

"Please," said Gareth.

Reluctantly Binny took hold of the black line on either side of the hook, remembered something she had been told once by a nurse, and cheered up immensely.

"Shut your eyes and it won't hurt!"

"What?"

"A nurse told me to do it once, before I had an injection. Only I didn't. But she promised it was true. Shut your eyes!"

"How can it possibly make any difference?" argued Gareth, but all the same, he shut his eyes and Binny pulled.

"AAARRRRHHH!" roared Gareth, but it had worked. His arm was free and the hook was out, with a fragment of Gareth's arm on the barb. Blood flooded, poured off Gareth's elbow, onto the rock, was lost amongst the bladderwrack, and reappeared at the waterline. Frantically Binny hunted for something, anything, that could possibly become a bandage. Her pockets contained nothing but fragments of sea-soaked tissue.

A sock.

Binny wrenched off her sneaker, saved it just in time from

rolling away down to the waves, tugged off a sock (pink-edged, soaked, not at all clean), folded it into a lump, and held it hard against the hole in Gareth's arm.

"What are you doing?" he asked, and she saw that once again his eyes were closed.

"Making it better," she said.

Chapter Eight

Aunty Violet's house had been used as a dumping place for all the things she did not want in her apartment in Spain. They were not nice things; it was easy to see why she had not wanted them. Binny and her family threw them away by the armload, and yet there always seemed to be more. Yellowing papers, chipped china, old clothes, pictures of people from long ago. The residue of many years, gathered together by Aunty Violet, piled into cupboards and forgotten.

A smell clung to these things, sweetish, musty.

"It's only damp," said Clem, but to Binny it was more than damp; it was Aunty Violet.

"She smelled more of cigarettes than anything," said Clem.

"Other things too, though," said Binny.

Clem found a perfume bottle, yellow dregs at the bottom. "Chanel," she said, "Number Five. Let's—"

"Don't!" shouted Binny, but too late. Binny fled the room choking, tasting Aunty Violet in the back of her mouth.

Clem threw the bottle away. "In the kitchen trash," she said later, and stared, puzzled, at the trash can, from which the bottle had vanished. "Oh," said Clem, and went back to her cupboard emptying. She found it quite an interesting job. The old photographs intrigued her, with their images of family now vanished. One in particular caught her eye and she brought it down for everyone to see.

The family laughed when they saw it, because it might have been Binny in a few years' time. Same crinkled seaweed hair. Same questioning eyes and crescent moon eyebrows. Same smile. Leaning against the harbor wall, hands on her hips, watching them.

Aunty Violet, age sixteen.

"She DOES NOT look like me!" snapped Binny, but except for the old-fashioned clothes, and the cigarette between her lips, she looked very like Binny.

Fascinatingly like.

"I don't smoke," said Binny primly. *I don't,* she added privately in her head, *but I could.*

Packets of cigarettes turned up in all sorts of odd corners in that house. Some with Spanish writing, some with English. Some half-full, some still sealed. As fast as they were found, they were bundled into the trash can, but always a new one appeared.

The morning after the people had come to the house next door, Binny, rummaging through a very unpleasant purple handbag, had found another.

Everyone was out. James with his mother. Clem buying paint for the kitchen cupboard doors. Binny opened the packet of Spanish cigarettes and sniffed. Quite nasty, although not, she decided, spraying her rescued perfume very cautiously in the direction of the open window, anything as bad as Chanel No. 5.

"I am the *opposite* of Aunty Violet!" said Binny out loud. "In every single possible way!"

She took a cigarette, posed, hands on her hips before the mirror, and gazed.

After a while she went downstairs for a box of matches.

She used quite a lot of them before she lit the cigarette, but at last, by actually setting fire to the end like a birthday cake candle, she managed it. The smoke made her eyes sting, and the smell was so strong she was forced to squirt more Chanel, to cover it up. All the same, she did not give up. She put it between her lips and stuck her head out of her bedroom window, in the time-honored manner of first-time secret smokers.

Almost at her elbow, somebody sniggered.

★ ★ ★

Binny jumped so hard with shock that the Chanel bottle dropped from her hand and smashed on the path below. There, almost close enough to touch, also leaning out of a bedroom window, was a boy.

Binny and the boy locked eyes, enemies before a word was spoken.

"Now I know what the stink was," said the boy, and he glanced from the broken perfume bottle to Binny's cigarette, no longer in her mouth, but still smoking horribly and perilously close to her hair.

"It was an experiment," said Binny coldly.

"What, like setting your head on fire?"

Binny hastily stuck the cigarette back in her mouth, raked her fingers through her scorched seaweed, and tried not to cough.

"How old are you, then?" asked the boy, and he asked it in a voice which showed that in his opinion Binny looked very young indeed.

"Older than you, I bet!" said Binny.

"Yeah? I'm thirteen!"

"I'm fourteen!"

"What a lie!"

"Look who's talking!"

Hot ash dropped on Binny's hand, and she squeaked in

surprise. The boy's eyes, dark behind his hideous spectacles, gleamed with mirth. Binny did the only thing possible. She reached out of her window and passed him first the packet of cigarettes, and then the box of matches.

"Dare you!" said Binny.

The boy managed the lighting of his cigarette with such ease that Binny was thankful he had not seen her birthday cake candle attempts. Afterward he pocketed both cigarettes and matches. Then he looked at Binny, and inhaled for a very long time.

It was a definite challenge.

Binny drank in smoke so deeply that for a moment it was as if the world went silent. Done it! she thought triumphantly, and then the pain hit. In the past she had inhaled some unpleasant substances: ice-cold Coke, shampoo bubbles, swimming pool water. None of those things were anything as bad. She choked. Her eyes burned. She clutched the windowsill and rocked backward and forward and her voice went "Urgh-urgh-urgh," just like when she was little and had asthma and they made her breathe into a paper bag.

The boy watched and did not attempt to conceal his delight. He was doing well, now on his second cigarette, and puffing so quickly he had already achieved his own cloud of smoke.

Suddenly, from inside his house, a woman's voice called, "Gareth!"

The boy Gareth froze.

"Gareth, are you in your room?"

He glanced over his shoulder, flapped momentarily at the smoke, realized it wouldn't work, climbed out onto his windowsill, turned, hung awkwardly by his hands for a moment, and dropped to the ground. The cottages were so low built that it was only a short drop, but still he did it with impressive calm, as if he had done the same thing many times before.

"Gareth!"

He moved very quickly, dark and thin and hurrying, rather like one of the earwigs that Binny had disturbed the previous day. Down the path he scuttled, and then over the fence by the apple tree into Binny's own garden. He looked like he'd done that before too.

"Gareth!"

Binny shot down the stairs, pulled open the back door of her own house, waved him inside, and pushed him out again by the front. They raced down the street together, free.

"You were lucky I was there," said Binny.

"You and your filthy cigarettes!"

"You were spying on us last night. My brother saw you."

"Yeah, and I saw you, staring in my window."

"It was a lot nicer before you came."

"It'll be a lot nicer when you're gone."

They reached the promenade that led to the harbor. Low chains hung between posts, guarding careless walkers from wandering over the edge. Gareth stepped over the chains and walked on the outside. Binny skipped past him to do the same, joggling him hard.

"Hey, that's my bad arm!" snapped Gareth.

"What's bad about it?" demanded Binny, pirouetting on the brink of a very large drop.

"I broke it a few weeks ago. It's just out of the cast."

"How did you do that? Falling out of bed?"

Gareth stopped still and stared at her. He went very red.

"You did!" exclaimed Binny. "You really did!" and she became helpless with laughter. "I got it right! That's what you did! Oh, I wish you could see your face!"

"It was a very high bed!" snarled Gareth. "It was a bunk bed, on a school trip. I forgot I was in it. I don't see why it's so funny. It's the sort of thing anyone might do."

Binny howled, doubled over.

The harbor pier jutted out from the promenade. Old stone, patched with concrete. A high wall on one side, a wide stretch of cobbles on the other, piled in places with lobster pots. Its edge was also guarded by hanging chains, except in the places where slimy green steps led down to the water. The harbor and the promenade made a right-angled corner. When the tide was out, as it was now, the hanging chains guarded a thirty-foot drop onto slime and rocks.

Gareth jostled past Binny, sprinted along the narrow space between the chains and the edge, and leaped the corner.

Binny stopped laughing.

Voices from the harbor shouted out in angry warning.

"Dare you!" called Gareth.

The only way to jump it was to do it very quickly. No hesitation, no glance down. Breathe. Run. Leap. Ten seconds, and it was done.

"Easy!" said Binny.

All around people were exclaiming with shock and indignation. Two fishermen left their rods to yell at them. Onlookers shook their children by their shoulders and said, "Don't you dare try anything like that!"

Only one face was not angry. Liam, the seal boat owner.

"When we were kids we did a lot worse," he remarked. "We used to play tag along the top of the harbor wall. Rode our bikes there too."

All the parents who heard closed their eyes in horror. All

the listening children clamored, "Why can't we do that?" The fishermen shrugged. The crowd dwindled as the children were hauled away to the safety of gift shops and ice cream.

Liam gave Binny an infinitesimally small wink.

She would have jumped a dozen harbor corners to see him do it again.

That did not happen. Liam, economical in every way, gave out his favors in strictly limited quantities: one free boat ride, one wink. He turned away so quickly that Binny had to run after him.

"Are you going out to the seals again today?"

"Twenty minutes or so," said Liam over his shoulder, without stopping. "As soon as I've grabbed a sandwich."

"Would it be all right if me and Gareth came too?"

Liam pulled a roll of pink tickets from his jeans pocket.

"Could we . . . could we . . . pay you later?"

"Don't think so," said Liam, very promptly.

"Oh. Perhaps Gareth . . ."

But Gareth had vanished. Binny ran along the pier, calling him, and then up and down the promenade, and out onto the sands, but he was nowhere to be found. Liam evaded her too, dodging out to sea with his latest cargo of sticky tourists while she was still hunting. Despite this, Binny went home feeling happier than she had for days.

She had jumped the harbor corner and not fallen in.

Liam had winked.

And there was Gareth.

Gareth.

At school all friendships had seethed with politics. At home there was always someone needing consideration: James to be forgiven, her mother to be protected, Clem to be worshipped with caution and handled with care.

Even Liam did not come without his heart-stopping price.

But with Gareth nothing was needed. No admiration, no tact, no caution, no politeness, no responsibility in any way. Never before had Binny had such a perfect companion: so handy, so alien, so entirely insensitive that she didn't have to bother about his feelings at all. Binny knew that Gareth would have cheerfully watched her fall into the harbor or choke on Spanish cigarette smoke. She knew, because she would have done the same to him.

"We're enemies," she explained to her mother.

"Don't be silly, Binny."

"It's true," said Binny.

She was still happy when she went to bed, but late in

the night she awoke and discovered that she was no longer happy at all.

"Oh! Oh! Oh!" wailed Binny.

"One of her states," murmured James, not bothering to wake, but Binny's mother and Clem, both bleary-eyed, came stumbling to the rescue.

"Mum! Clem! Someone!"

"All right, Binny! All right now. Just a dream."

"No, no, I've done something awful."

"Of course you haven't."

"Can I go to the doctor's? Can I go to the hospital?"

"Perhaps, in the morning, if you still want to. Lie down now."

"You've got to listen," sobbed Binny.

"Mmm?"

"Aunty Violet's cigarettes."

"Yes?"

"I tried them."

"That was silly."

"And now I can feel the black!"

"The black?"

"It's like tar. It sticks inside you. We learned it at school."

"How many of Aunty Violet's cigarettes did you smoke, Binny?"

"Nearly a whole one."

"That's it, then, you're dead," said Clem, who was not always angelic, and went back to bed.

"*Please* can I go to the hospital, *please*?"

"You can have a glass of water," said her mother, and went to fetch her one.

"What will it do?"

"It will calm you down."

"What about the black?"

"Are you planning to smoke any more of Aunty Violet's cigarettes?"

"No, no. They're terrible. No."

"Then drink this water and the black won't be a problem."

Binny snuffled her way through the glass of water and remembered her enemy.

"What about if I'd smoked two?" she asked.

"Well. I suppose that would be twice as bad. But you haven't smoked two, have you?"

"No."

"And you don't plan to?"

"No."

"Night, night, then, Binny."

"I broke the bottle of scent stuff, too."

"It couldn't matter less."

"Oh..."

"Back to sleep now."

Binny's eyes closed and when she woke again it was bright morning and there was Gareth with his head sticking out of his bedroom window. She was so pleased to see him still alive that she thought enemy or not, maybe she did have to care a little bit about him after all. It was bad enough having the death of Aunty Violet on her conscience. Another accidental calamity would be more than she could bear.

Water.

That was the cure.

Binny filled a glass from the bathroom tap and held it out to Gareth.

"Drink this."

"Not likely."

"It's just water."

"I'm not drinking it."

"Please."

"Please," imitated Gareth.

"All right," said Binny, losing patience. "Dare you."

"What?"

"Double dare," said Binny relentlessly.

Gareth gave her a look of loathing, reached out from his window, took the glass, and drank.

"What's the idea?" he demanded afterward. "It's just water."

"I know. That's what I told you. Now drink another. You can fill it up with your own water if you like."

"I think you're insane."

"Just do it."

"No."

"All right. I'll tell your mum you were smoking."

"You'll have a job. She's more than two hundred miles away."

"Who was that calling you yesterday, then?"

"Mind your own," said Gareth, but all the same, and eyeing Binny suspiciously as he did it, he drank another glass of water.

The woman whose voice Binny had heard was not Gareth's mother, or even his stepmother. She was his father's girl-friend. Monstrously selfish. Determined to ruin Gareth's life, and only interested in Gareth's father because she was after his money.

Said Gareth.

Much to everyone's surprise, Gareth had appeared at

the kitchen door almost as soon as breakfast was over that morning looking slightly irritated, as if he had been summoned.

"Well, come in!" Binny's mother had smiled, and he had come in, said, "Oh, you're there!" to Binny, and completely ignored everyone else. Now the two of them were up in her cupboard-sized bedroom watching the nightmare money-grabbing girlfriend prowl round the next-door garden as if she owned it. Pausing to look at a butterfly. Sniffing a rose.

"Who does she think she is?" asked Gareth crossly. "My mum planted that rose."

"Where is your mum?"

"Oxford. She lives there. So do I, in school-time. Vacations I spend with Dad. And now Her. Old witch."

"Why, if you hate her so much?" demanded Binny. "Why didn't you stay in Oxford with your mum?"

"They tricked me, that's why," said Gareth bitterly. "We used to come here when I was little. It's my grandfather's house, really; he rents it out except when the family want it. We stopped coming when Mum and Dad split. Dad said we ought to try other places. Mucky old France, and rotten Scotland. Rome, and you chuck a coin in a fountain if you want to come back. Ha! You wouldn't believe how many people do that!"

"I did once," said Binny, nodding.

"You!"

"Yes, before——"

But Gareth was not interested in any past worlds but his own. He hurried on with his story. "Anyway, wherever we went I kept saying it was rubbish and we should come back here, and at last Dad said we could and I was really pleased and then, with zero notice, he tells me *she's* coming too. Her!"

Binny craned her head out of the window for a closer look.

"Is she really that bad?"

"Don't you believe me? She's beyond evil. Look at her messing about with that rose!"

"Watering it," said Binny fairly.

"That's what she wants you to think! Oh well! I've got a plan to drive them mad. It won't be hard; my dad's got a really bad temper. There's only so much he can stand. I've already tried hitching. I did that last night, but some mad old biddy called the police. So I'm going to make them *send* me home!"

"I can't see why they want to keep you here for a minute," said Binny frankly. "Anyway, I'm not staying in any longer. I'm going to see my sister's kitten. Her friend's giving it to her as soon as it's big enough to leave its mother. We go and visit it so it gets to know us. You can come if you like."

"You'd better not let Her see it," said Gareth. "She hates cats. And dogs. Hates them."

"I bet you're just saying that to be nasty."

"Don't believe me if you like. You'll soon find out . . ." Gareth paused, stared, and burst out laughing.

"What?" demanded Binny.

"Look at your brother!"

Binny looked where Gareth was pointing, and there was James, obviously supposing himself to be unobserved, behaving disgracefully in a corner of the garden.

"What's he doing?" she wailed.

"Seeing how high he can get it up the fence, of course," said Gareth, and he called, "Oy! Lean backward! Further than that!"

James glanced up at him, nodded, leaned impossibly far, momentarily achieved a wonderful new height, and fell flat on his back. Binny stormed down to yell at him, but was overtaken by Gareth, so that by the time she arrived a technical discussion was in progress.

"I ran out!"

"You were too close anyway. It's all about the angle."

She went off to visit the kitten alone.

Chapter Nine

James was having a wonderful summer. Every day he woke up fizzing. Every night he fell asleep gloating. The endless days of school and the dingy city apartment had almost faded from his mind. They had been replaced by much more interesting things. Sunlight, old ladies, and his private tally of high tide marks on the garden fence. His wonderful wetsuit. The sea. Every day, at least once, he would head for the beach, march solemnly into the shallows, crouch where the water was about knee-deep, gasp at the next engulfing wave, and then run shrieking to whoever he had stationed with towels on the sand. That was the highlight of his day, but he had many other pleasures. Beneath his bed a snail collection had tripled in number. Outside his bedroom window his hanging basket of stolen lettuce seeds was thick and green.

"And poison," whispered James, very quietly, so that no one heard. James watered his lettuce with a variety of awful liquids brewed with great secrecy in his sand pie bucket. Yesterday moldy tomato juice water. Today he had some seagull poo to experiment with. Tomorrow, tomorrow. . . James hugged himself at the thought of all the tomorrows.

"You're supposed to eat lettuce when it gets as big as yours," remarked Binny one morning.

James gave her a great and knowing glance. "You can if you like," he said.

Binny left the lettuce unpicked.

As well as all this, James had the old ladies in the old people's home where his mother had found her new job.

James and the old ladies got on very well indeed.

The old ladies lived lives of delicious selfishness. The ways they thought and the way James thought were so exactly alike that he felt at home there from the first. Nothing they did surprised him, and nothing he did surprised them. They called him: "Mr. Marvelous," "Kip," "My lovely." In return he learned their familiar playground names: Maisie, Ruby, Ella, Grace,

Quite often, but never too often for James, his mother took him to work with her in the mornings. Binny and Clem waved them off from the doorstep. James's pink and green wetsuit glowed in the early sunshine.

"He looks like one of those frogs," said Binny. "You know, the sort that live in rainforests and hunters mash them up to make deadly poison for their arrows. It's funny how pleased he always is to go with Mum."

"It's not just the old people he likes there," said Clem. "It's the chickens as well."

The chickens belonged to the old people's home. They lived in a luxurious chicken house on the edge of the lawn. On his last visit James had been allowed to retrieve an egg.

"A real egg," he told Binny. "Not out of a supermarket. Out of a *real* chicken's *real* bum."

"Yuk," said Binny, but James, who had eaten the egg with a sort of ravenous glee, did not agree. Now he wanted his own chickens.

"Yes, wouldn't they be lovely?" agreed his mother when she heard this latest desire.

"Now?" asked James.

"No, no, when you're grown up," said his mother, hurrying him along the twisty streets. "When you're a farmer."

"I'm a farmer now. Except I've only got plastic animals and those snails and a toad I can't find."

"He's probably happier being a free-range toad."

"It's chickens I want most. Do you think the old ladies might give me one of theirs?"

"Of course not! Why should they?"

"They do give me things. Loads of things. Last time I came, all of them gave me things all day."

That was true. Once the old ladies discovered James's eager acceptance of anything offered they treated him like a brightly colored, animated trash can.

He was very polite.

"Oh, thank you!" he said, to cookies, sugar lumps, magazines to cut pictures from, ends of chocolate bars, ancient notebooks, worn-out pens, and unpleasantly freckled bananas.

"I don't care for bananas when they go like that," said one old lady. James didn't care for them when they went like that either, but he gravely accepted them all the same.

"Nice manners," said the old ladies approvingly.

Sometimes they showed him their treasures. Ella had a toffee tin full of watches. "That was my mother's," she told James, tipping them into his eager little hands. "My husband's, my dad's. That one's very old. It was my grandfather's. He was a tin miner. That's what they gave him for fifty years down the mine."

"Just that?"

"You're right. It was an insult. Put it out of sight."

"Now then, Mr. Marvelous," said Maisie who was brisk and bossy. "Hold out your hand."

It was a large red stone, warm and strangely light. Color spilled from its shadow.

"There's a thing," said Maisie, and James nodded solemnly. There was a thing. No doubt about that.

Once or twice he was told stories.

"You wouldn't remember my husband, Kip. No. So you'd not remember his mother. No. She died with her fists closed tight. That was her nature. Never let it be yours."

James's fists were not closed tight. Far from it.

"One of the old ladies gave me fifty pence," he told his mother the next morning, skipping as he remembered. "First she gave me a dirty old purse thing because she said I could put my money in it. Then she gave me fifty pence because I hadn't got any."

"You shouldn't have taken it. If anyone else offers you money you must say, 'Thank you very much, but I'm afraid I'm not allowed.'"

"Fifty pence isn't much. She had pounds and pounds. She had to tip all the pounds out of her purse to find the fifty pence for me."

"James," said his mother, pausing in the street to make sure he was listening. "Did you completely understand what I said to you about taking money from the old ladies?"

"No," said James cheerfully.

"Well, then, I'll tell you again. No taking money. Not even fifty pence."

"Not even a pound?"

"No."

"Not even five or ten or twenty or a hundred pounds?"

"No. Money. At. All!" said his mother very firmly. "Now, then, here we are! What did you bring to play with?"

James flapped about his bag of plastic sheep.

"Lovely."

"Do they like me? The old ladies?"

"Yes, very much indeed."

"They'd better not kiss me."

"Scoot into the garden. Nobody will kiss you there."

James scooted, and set up his sheep farm as close as he could to the chickens. He built pebble walls to enclose a field of fat lambs and their mothers, a pebble mountain for the curly-horned ram, and a track for the tractor to come and go.

"On a real farm," Binny had told him once, more than a bit wistfully, "you'd have a black and white sheep dog to round up those sheep."

"I'd rather have a quad bike," said James.

He had made one from Lego, and when his mother

appeared with mid-morning orange juice and cookies, he was driving it through his fields, separating out the fattest lambs to load into his little trailer.

"Where are they going?" asked his mother and she smiled down at him because he had played alone so nicely, for so long, and had been so much admired from the windows as she worked.

James buzzed secretly in her ear.

"Off to the butchers!"

"James!"

Back at home, with James away, the house felt empty. Binny sought out Clem, who was in the garden brushing her hair into a sheaf of silver-gold.

"What are you going to do now James has gone, Clem? Paint?"

"Nope."

"Why not?"

"I can have one day off, can't I?"

"I suppose," admitted Binny. Clem's painting of the kitchen had been so successful that secretly Binny would have liked to keep her attached to a paintbrush until the whole house was transformed.

"I'm playing my flute," said Clem.

"All day?"

"Perhaps."

"But what about me?"

Clem gave her a considering look. There was a change-in-the-weather note in her sister's voice. A small cloud. A need to be needed.

"You could go and see Kate if you're tired of the beach and the harbor," she suggested. "Or carry on with clearing the garden. You're doing so well out there! You could make a cake for a surprise for Mum and James. Or . . ."

"It doesn't matter," said Binny, stiffly.

"Binny . . ."

"Go and play your flute."

"What about a run down to the sea first? Both of us? Before it gets too crowded?"

"No, thank you."

"What, then?"

"Nothing."

Clem waited.

"I wish you'd go and play your flute," said Binny.

"'Smatter, Bin?"

"I am perfectly all right," said Binny with dignity, stalked upstairs, and flung herself down on her bed.

Her mood was suddenly in free fall, a state she knew all

too well. A heaviness inside. A hollow loneliness. A need to either quarrel or cry. A downward plunge that could only be escaped by a huge loss of temper, howling for her mother, or what people like teachers called going too far.

Trouble on the way.

Then Binny heard her enemy. The boy next door. Sudden voices came clearly through her open bedroom window. He was in trouble too.

Binny rolled onto her bedroom floor, rested her cheek on her windowsill, and listened.

Gareth and an angry man. Clearly his father.

"You are NOT going to spoil this day, Gareth!"

"I won't, if you go without me."

"That's not what we want."

"She wants, you mean!" Binny heard Gareth say scornfully. "Her! She's the boss around here!"

"Gareth," said the man, in a voice tight with patience. "Come on! Give it a go! Alice spent a fortune on those helicopter tickets, just to please you."

"She could please me for free if she'd just get lost."

"Right!" snapped Gareth's father. "That's enough! Stop arguing and get yourself dressed!"

"Dressed?"

"Yes! Dressed! Not those things you've worn for the last

forty-eight hours straight! Put on a clean shirt for a start! DON'T shrug like that at me! You must have one! Here!"

The sound of drawers bumping open and closed came then, a growl of protest from Gareth, a very ominous silence, and an explosion.

"Where did you get these from?"

"Mind your own!"

"You didn't buy them around here!"

"So?"

"I thought I smelled smoke the other day! I would have come and checked if Alice hadn't stopped me!"

"I said she was the boss around here," commented Gareth.

"Right!" bellowed Gareth's father, suddenly becoming very noisy. "Off that bed! Into that shower! Get some clean clothes on and get yourself downstairs!"

"Or?" Binny heard Gareth ask.

"There is no *or*," replied his father and slammed out of the room.

Then there was silence.

"Gareth!" Binny called softly out of the window.

"What d'you want?"

"I think you'd better do as he says!"

"You mind your own!" snapped Gareth, but after that there was no longer silence. There was the sound of the shower running, and afterward somebody stamping around, dragging on clothes. A few minutes later, when Binny heard footsteps on the stairs, she could not resist hurrying across to James's room to look down onto the street.

She was just in time. Gareth, a thin fair woman, and an angry-faced man. Every inch of Gareth looked like he was sulking. Every inch of the thin woman looked braced for disaster. Every inch of Gareth's father looked stiff with temper as he herded them both up the street toward the garage around the corner where he kept his enormous and immaculate car.

Just as they turned out of sight, Binny saw the cigarettes Gareth's father had taken from Gareth fall unnoticed from his jacket pocket. For no good reason except that they had once been hers, she darted down the stairs and out of the house to retrieve them. Exactly at the moment that she picked them up, Gareth's father reappeared.

"Forgot the blasted tickets!" Binny heard him call over his shoulder. "Carry on! I'll catch up with you!"

Then he almost knocked into Binny, squarely in front of him and clutching Aunty Violet's cigarettes.

"I don't think you want those," he said, in a very bossy don't-keep-me-waiting voice, and he held out his hand.

"They're mine," said Binny, and shifted them behind her back.

"I found them, not ten minutes ago, in my son's bedroom," said Gareth's father, "and so, young lady, I think you'd better give them to me."

Binny, above all things, hated to be called "young lady." It was an Aunty Violet way of talking. It was unbearable.

"No wonder Gareth's so nasty," she said.

Gareth's father managed to ignore this remark. "I am waiting," he said coldly, still with his hand held out, "for you to do as I have asked."

Usually she would have given in, but this was Binny on her downward plunge, going too far.

"I don't see why I should."

"I can't imagine your mother knows you have those things!"

"She does!" said Binny very triumphantly indeed. "So!" And for good measure she added a phrase she had learned very recently from Gareth himself. "Mind your own!"

"WHAT did you say?" thundered Gareth's father.

"Mind your own!" said Binny, and then she skittered off down the cobbled street singing, "Mind your own! Mind your own!" Without looking back she knew he was staring after her. She could feel his outraged, vanquished glare hot between her shoulder blades.

I won! she thought, skipping. The morning seemed

suddenly illuminated as Binny, the human pendulum, swung with lovely reckless bravery upward into the light.

"You'll be late for your helicopter!" she called happily over her shoulder as she turned out of his sight, and then she headed for the harbor. She jumped the corner of the harbor wall for nothing more than pleasure, her shadow a small blue kite at her feet, and ran straight to Liam.

"Oh, it's you," said Liam.

He was mopping. He always fanatically cleaned his boat after each batch of sticky seal watchers. He liked to eliminate all traces of them. In an ideal world he would have taken their money at the harbor wall and never let them aboard at all.

"I could do that," offered Binny.

Liam looked up, surprised.

"I could mop. And pick up the rubbish. And wipe round the edge where they put their hands! Then you could have a rest."

"Do I look tired?"

Binny looked. Liam did not look tired. He looked like a brand-new delivery from the Truly Awesome shop. "No," she admitted. "You look . . . you look like a . . ." She suddenly remembered her last term at school, when they had done the Egyptians and all their pyramids and princes.

"You look like a sun god!" she told him triumphantly.

"A sun dog?" asked Liam, considerably startled.

"God," corrected Binny. "A sun god! But..."

"What?"

"Mopping."

That made Liam pause, because he was not just a good-natured, super-economical, hygiene-obsessed exploiter of seals and tourists. He was also honest. So although he understood quite clearly why Binny had likened him to a sun god, he also saw why she looked at his mop the way she did. He did not enjoy mopping, even though he was very good at it. It was not his image. Surfing, yes. Mopping, no.

"Come on down then," he said, and he smiled and held out a hand, but Binny was already at his feet.

Liam became very brisk. "Wipe off the seats. Wipe off the handrails. Put the candy wrappers and stuff in that bag. Check for chewing gum under the benches. We'll be off as soon as I can get rid of another batch of tickets."

"Me too?"

"Well. I'll see how you get on."

The pendulum that was Binny settled down into a quiet tick of contentment. The last hour of storms and drama faded like a dream. The Spanish cigarettes went into the bag with all the rest of the rubbish. She settled down to become indispensable.

That second seal trip was far better than Binny's first. This time the local colony of seals were not on the rocks just across the bay from the harbor. Nor were they anywhere around the island that floated, looking like a badly wrapped parcel, a couple of miles out to sea. Liam, horribly conscious of the twin values of time and fuel, circled it with increasing gloom, pausing the engine at all the places where the seals were usually to be seen.

"What'll you do if you can't find any?" whispered Binny, as he peered into yet another empty corner, and she looked anxiously at the seal hungry holidaymakers who had paid so much. "Give them their money back?"

"Shut up!" hissed Liam, glancing over to his passengers, clearly dreading that any of them had heard this horrible suggestion.

"I only—"

"Just shut it!" ordered Liam. "We'll go over to the point. If they're not across the bay or out at the island, that's where they'll be."

"How far's the point?"

"Too far."

It wasn't really. It took not much more than ten minutes, and then there were the seals, seven of them, smiling their teddy bear smiles, lolling on the rocks, not looking at all guilty about all the fuel it had taken to find them.

"Ooohh!" exclaimed the holidaymakers, reaching for their cameras.

"Here," said Liam, and he handed Binny a bucket, half-full of chunks of old and smelly mackerel. "Throw a few out. Not the whole lot."

"Me?" asked Binny, amazed.

"Yep."

"Oh, thank you! Thank you!" said Binny.

It was hard to believe that a day that had begun so badly could end so well. Binny went home to her family feeling very pleased with herself indeed, and James sniffed the dead mackerel smell on his sister's hands with admiration and envy.

Binny's mother was less happy.

"Who exactly is this boy?" she demanded.

"It's Kate's brother," said Clem. "He's all right. I've met him. He runs the seal boat in the summer to earn money for university. He's not going to kidnap Binny. He hasn't got time."

"He may not have time to kidnap her," said Binny's mother, "but it wouldn't take five minutes to drown her."

"Mum!" protested Binny. "I got the *swimming* prize, remember!"

"Yes, and I'm very pleased you did," said her mother, "but all the same I'm going down to the harbor for a little chat with Kate's brother."

"A chat about what?"

"Life jackets," said her mother. "Has he got life jackets? He ought to have, if he's taking passengers out to sea."

"He's got a great big smelly box of them in the middle of the boat," said Binny crossly. "They're all stiff and they look mildewy and no one ever puts them on. And he's got a first aid box and a disinfectant spray and two orange life preservers like they have on the harbor. So it's perfectly safe, even if I do fall in. Which I won't."

"That's wonderful," said her mother, but she still went down to see Liam. She felt she could not rest until she had explained to him that if he was ever so generous as to let Binny onto his boat again, she must wear a life jacket, even for mopping the deck when they were tied to the harbor wall.

"Mum!" moaned Binny.

"No problem," said Liam cheerfully, and he let Binny's mother come aboard and help Kate, who happened to be with him, sort out a life jacket in Binny's size from the great

big smelly box. Binny watched them from the harbor with a very mutinous expression until Kate transformed the hideous orange water-stained garment by writing on the front and back in big black letters.

CREW

"Just in case a passenger wants to borrow it when you need it," explained Kate, but Binny was still charmed.

"Crew!" she said.

"Liam won't want you every day," warned her mother as they made their way home. "He can't be that busy. His prices are appalling!"

"I know," agreed Binny. "Four pounds fifty! Seven if you're grown up! Or twenty-five for a family ticket with up to three children. Trips last no more than an hour. Guaranteed to see the seals. Photo opportunities after."

"What sort of photo opportunities?"

"Standing beside Liam."

That was how Binny became part of the crew. Wiping down. Mopping. Trash picking. Counting change. Rationing the mackerel. Rinsing out the bucket. Saying "Good-bye, good-bye" to the customers at the end of a trip, and looking wistful beside the cookie tin labeled COMFORTS FOR THE CREW.

Not that Binny was ever given a share of the comforts. Her reward for all her hard work was to exist in Liam's shining presence.

A scruffy little satellite racing round a very bright sun.

Chapter Ten

Gradually the Cornwallis family was transforming Aunty Violet's house. First the kitchen, then the living room. All in one weekend Clem and her mother painted the walls, scrubbed the blackened fireplace to rose-colored brick, and tore up the hideous carpet and admired the pale gold flagstones underneath. While they did this, Binny emptied the cupboards on either side of the window. They were full of old letters, bills, and receipts. Binny searched them carefully, braving the smell to turn pages and shake open dusty envelopes. She didn't say what she was doing, but they knew.

"Binny," said her mother after a while. "I understand now that I should have tried to find out what happened to him. I wish I had. Only at the time . . ."

"I know," said Binny.

At the time. Their father just dead, the family bankrupt, home gone, and a move across the country. Winter, and always somebody ill. Binny's asthma, James's chest. Clem's sadness. Learning to live without a car. Day after day of Clem collecting Binny from school and the trudge home together to the empty apartment. Unlocking the door with the key that Clem carried like a weight all day, such was her fear of losing it. On those days it would be black dark before their mother got home from work with James, and still supper to be cooked and reading books heard and bathtime and stories and clothes for tomorrow.

Also new raw awareness of what they had, and didn't have.

"Practice your flute now, Clem, before anyone's trying to get little ones to sleep."

"Binny, where is your sweater? You mustn't, you can't, not even to be kind, lend clothes to people at school."

James's soaked boots to be dried with a hair dryer.

That was how it had been, and why, when they finally heard of Aunty Violet's mission from Spain to rescue poor beset Granny, except for Binny's shrieks and tantrums, there had been nothing done at all.

For Binny's mother, all mixed in with the dismay and guilt, the news had been a sort of relief. It would be better for Granny and better for Max. She had waited for Binny to allow him to fade from their lives. It had not happened. More than two years later, and here she was, still wanting him back.

"What if Aunty Violet didn't even bother to take him to a rescue center?" she asked. "She said he went to another home, but she might just have made that up. What if she just dumped him?"

"She would never have done that," said Clem.

"What if she took him to the vet's," suggested James. "In my class where we lived before, there was a girl and she had a dog and the dog was called Holly and one day they took Holly to the vet's because of all the pooing in the house and do you know what the vet did?"

"I don't think we want to hear this silly story, thank you, James!" said his mother very firmly.

"'S not a silly story," said James. "It's a sad story. It's a MURDER story..."

James's mother came very quickly down her ladder, picked up James round his waist like a roll of carpet, and left the room. They heard footsteps on the stairs. They heard James's bedroom door bang shut. Then she came back again and said very calmly, "Binny, no vet would put to sleep a young, healthy dog."

"She knows that," said Clem. "Don't you, Binny?"

Binny, who had become very hunched in her corner, did not reply.

"I'm going out for bread," continued her mother. "Come

with me, Binny, and help choose everyone ice creams for a treat?"

"No, thank you."

"I would love ice cream," said Clem helpfully.

"So would I," agreed her mother. "I'll get everyone's favorites. Chocolate for you, Binny, mint for Clem. Coffee for me. What about James?"

"Anything as long as it's covered in strawberry sauce," said Clem.

"James!" exclaimed Binny crossly. In disgrace, or out of it, he always had the best.

"Spoiled," agreed Clem when their mother had gone. "It's our fault! We did it! Doesn't this room look better? I wonder what Aunty Violet would say."

Binny glanced uneasily at the photograph of Aunty Violet, age sixteen, currently regarding them from the windowsill. Aunty Violet. They were always moving her to new locations. Wherever they put her, she did not look right.

"I think she's angry," said Binny, and then she asked what she had wanted to ask for weeks. "Clem, do you ever see her?"

"See her? Aunty Violet?"

"The day we moved here I saw her. Just for a moment. Her face, like a reflection."

"Binny. You know you didn't. I expect it *was* a reflection."

"No."

"She's gone, Bin."

"I don't think so. I think she's here."

"She died far away in Spain. That was the place that mat-
tered to her. Not England. Not here. I can't imagine her
here. Why would she want to be, even if she could?"

Because I am here, thought Binny, but she did not speak
the words aloud. She did not want to answer the questions
that they would bring.

Why you?

I am the one that wished her dead.

I am the reason we are here.

I am the person who was sent the message.

Particular regards!

Clem was looking at Binny. She said, very gently, "Binny.
She's dead."

"I know she's dead!" yelled Binny. "But what sort of
dead? Plain dead? Dead in heaven? Dead, but does haunting? Are you laughing, Clem?"

"No. Not really."

"Answer me, then!"

"I would say plain dead," said Clem, as gravely as she
could. "There's Mum at the door. Eat your ice cream and
don't worry her. Hello, James!"

"Hello, don't kiss me," said James, his face a mixture of woefulness and hope. "Is the red one mine? Sorry, Binny. Mum said I could come down if I said sorry. That was it."

"It wasn't much," said his mother. "But I suppose it will have to do. Take that ice cream into the garden before you drip all over the floor. It's going to be a lovely evening. I think we should all go down to the beach."

"Do you think Aunty Violet ever went down to the beach?" asked Binny.

"I'm sure she did. I hope she did. I expect she knew the whole town."

Binny expected she did too. How strange, she thought, that Clem could not imagine her in this place. She herself could imagine Aunty Violet everywhere, and the more she thought about her, the clearer she became. A creak on the stairs at night. A breath of perfume. A whiff of smoke. Sometimes, as Binny walked the streets, she almost caught glimpses. A movement behind a window, or a stare, and there was Aunty Violet, all but visible.

Can she hear? wondered Binny suddenly, and after the others had followed James into the garden, she waited behind. Then she picked up the photograph from the windowsill, gripped it tight in both hands, and demanded, fiercely and desperately, *"What did you do with my dog?"*

Chapter Eleven

"You said you were going to build a tree house," James reminded Binny the following day, so she built one, all in a morning.

"Is that it?" he asked when she slid down the apple tree and announced that it was complete.

"Yes," said Binny, and she looked up with satisfaction at her achievement, which was no more than the broken surfboard, wedged high in the tree and tied into place with washing line.

"It looks like a boat in the sky," remarked her mother.

"A shipwreck in a tree, more like," said Clem.

The surfboard was not quite straight, and no matter how tightly Binny pulled her knots, it jerked a little when any weight was put on it. It was quite startling at first, and then pleasant. Exciting.

"Come up!" she invited her mother and Clem and James.

One by one they climbed into the apple tree, sat carefully

down on the surfboard, felt it lurch beneath them, and managed not to shriek.

"You can lie down if you like," offered Binny. "There's millions of room."

So as not to disappoint her each in turn bravely lay down, closed their eyes, and said, "Oh yes, lovely." After that they climbed as quickly as possible down to solid ground again, and nothing Binny could say would induce them to come back.

"It's perfectly safe!" she called down hopefully. "Come and look! If you stand on tiptoe you can nearly see the sea!"

"No, thank you, Binny!" they called back. "You can nearly see the sea from almost anywhere around here!"

Gareth didn't like Binny's tree house either. He came round that afternoon to look, intrigued by all the rustling, but he was not impressed. It reminded him far too much of the bunk bed from which he had fallen and broken his arm. He lay down, expecting disaster, and Binny gave him a rather harder experience of the exciting wobble than she had given any of her family.

"OY!" yelled Gareth, clutching at leaves.

"One night I might sleep up here," said Binny, showing off.

"You'd roll over and fall out."

"I'd tie myself on."

"Your mum would never let you."

Binny thought that was probably true, so she changed the subject.

"Did you really go up in a helicopter?"

"No," said Gareth with immense satisfaction. "*And* Dad got a speeding ticket trying to get there in time. Dead good! And then we missed it! Double good! So then She went all *Cry, cry, it's all my fault, I should have planned things better*, and he went ballistic."

Binny was appalled. "It was partly my fault," she admitted.

"I know, Dad said," agreed Gareth.

"He did?"

"Said you held him up. And about your incredible insolence. Well done!"

"Don't say that!" moaned Binny.

"Why not? I wish I'd heard you! Here he comes now, you can do it again if you like!"

Binny shrank back amongst the leaves in alarm as Gareth's father appeared, standing in the open door of his house, carrying an enormous bag and talking over his shoulder to somebody inside.

"You're not scared of him, are you?" asked Gareth scornfully.

"Of course not!" replied Binny, but all the same, she skidded as quickly as she could down from her surfboard and made a rush for her own kitchen door.

"Do you think he saw us?" she asked Gareth, who had followed almost as fast.

"Who cares?" replied Gareth, polishing apple-tree green from his glasses and looking inquisitively around. "Where is everyone?"

"James and Mum are down at the beach. Clem's upstairs. Where was your dad going?"

The huge bag Gareth's father had been carrying had worried Binny. Was he moving out? And if so, was it due to the disastrous helicopter day? Was this going to be another thing that was her fault?

"Going?" asked Gareth.

"He had a great big bag."

"Oh!" Gareth gave a snort of laughter. "He plays golf. That was for golf."

"All that?"

"Yep. He's got a flat pack golf course in that bag."

"What?"

"One of those you unroll on the beach."

"Wow!"

"Astroturf. Of course, you have to dig your own holes."

Binny's face became incredulous, then indignant, and then she grinned, a bit reluctantly.

"You believed me!" said Gareth, very pleased with himself, and then a new sound came, and it was his turn to be surprised. "What's that?"

It was Clem's flute. A few clear notes. A scale and then a glitter of arpeggios, rising and falling like a wave.

"Cool," said Gareth, unexpectedly pleasantly, and then spoiled it by looking around and remarking, "I can't believe this is really your kitchen."

"Why can't you?" asked Binny.

"It's a bit small. Compared."

"Compared to what?"

"To ours," said Gareth. "Is that another room through there?"

"Yes," said Binny sarcastically. "And it's supposed to be the living room. Those are supposed to be stairs and if you go up them, a place that's supposed to be a bathroom. You've already seen my bedroom. I suppose you guessed what it was?"

"Hello!" said Clem, appearing as Binny spoke. "It's Gareth from next door, isn't it?"

Clem was dressed entirely in black, tight black jeans, equally tight black top. Silver light reflected from her hair and ran along the flute she held in one hand. She gazed down from the top of the staircase at Gareth, and his mouth fell open and stayed that way.

"We were just talking about the house," said Binny. "He thinks it's a bit small."

"It is a bit small," agreed Clem. "Perhaps he could give us a hand enlarging it. Pushing back the walls or something. That be all right, Gareth?"

Still staring, Gareth shook his head. There was something about Clem that was out of his world. He had no knowledge of such people, past school age but not yet scornable adult. So flawless they seemed to radiate a cool light. Possessed of such a power that had she said "Kneel" his knees would have buckled on the spot.

Luckily she didn't. She merely asked, in a how-soon-am-I-going-to-get-rid-of-you kind of way, "What are you two doing this afternoon, then?"

"I'm going to Kate's," said Binny. "Gareth can come with me if he likes."

"Who's Kate?" asked Gareth, finding his voice, now that it was only Binny speaking.

"She's Clem's friend. Her family has that big café with all the tables outside, down near the harbor. She lets me clear the outside tables: wipe them clean, and take in the cups and things. Then if there's any money, I can keep it. There quite often is. Especially if people's kids have made a mess."

"You clean tables for tips?" asked Gareth.

"What's wrong with that?"

Only the silent presence of Clem prevented Gareth from saying what was wrong with that. Even so, his expression was so horrified that Binny offered another suggestion.

"Or I could go to Kate's on my own later, and we could go out on the seal boat. But you'd need four pounds fifty. How much have you got?"

"Mind your own!"

"I only asked because you'd have to pay. I don't have to because I'm crew."

"You!"

"I've got a special life jacket. CREW, it says."

"Whatever," said Gareth rudely.

"It's true, isn't it, Clem?"

"Yes it is, actually," said Clem, looking at Gareth with dislike.

"The seals are lovely," Binny told him. "Not a bit like fish!"

"Like fish?" asked Gareth, looking quite stupefied at this ignorance. "Of course they're not like fish! They're *not* fish! Anyway, I'm not going on any boats and I'm not cleaning tables for tips either..."

All the same, he found himself following Binny as she hurried outside. It was not a very successful expedition, however. At Kate's the tables were clean and empty. At the harbor the seal boat was just moving away.

"So much for your bright ideas," said Gareth. "I'm going out on my bike."

"Have you a bike?" asked Binny eagerly. "Did you hear Liam say the other day that he used to ride his along the harbor w—"

"I'm not going that way," said Gareth hastily, because if anyone was going to dare anyone else to ride along the harbor wall, it was he who was going to dare Binny, not the other way round. "I'm going nowhere near the harbor. I'm going . . ."

He paused.

"Where?" asked Binny.

A streak of dusty gold caught Gareth's eye. The moorland above the town was bright with yellow gorse. It was also a good safe distance from the harbor wall.

"Up there," he said, pointing.

"I've never been that way," said Binny, looking pleased. "How many bikes do you have?"

"One."

"We'll have to share, then."

"Share?" asked Gareth incredulously. So far he had managed to live his whole life without willingly sharing anything and he had no intention of changing that. "Are you mad? Anyway," he added thankfully, "it's a boy's bike. You couldn't even get started."

It was not just a boy's bike, it was a wonderful bike. It had everything. Suspension. Disc brakes. Twenty-one gears. It had cost eight hundred pounds, Gareth informed Binny (who nearly fell off it laughing at this blatant lie).

There was no question about Binny not even getting started. Starting was easy. Gareth had allowed her one try in order to prove that she couldn't do it, and she had taken off and left him racing breathlessly behind. Stopping was harder. At first the only way that she could manage it was by allowing herself to topple into the nearest convenient bush. Gareth found this so funny that he stopped complaining, and soon without even noticing, found himself not only sharing, but watching for traffic and calling helpful instructions.

Once they were out of the town, they took turns, in a manner invented by Binny and Clem long before. One would ride ahead, while the other hurried behind on foot. After a few minutes the rider would discard the bike, and go on foot themselves. Presently the one behind would collect it and overtake the other. It was much faster than walking, and in a very little time they were on the moor, where the sandy tracks were lined with prickly, coconut-smelling gorse. It was uncomfortable stuff to ride into accidentally, which happened quite often to both of them, Gareth because his newly mended arm felt so unexpectedly fragile that he had to ride one-handed to rest it, and Binny because the bike was much too big for her. To manage, she either had to stand on the pedals, or catch them with her feet as they flew past. It was a relief to both of them when they reached the highest point and had an excuse to stop and rest. Binny looked around at the wide spread of sunlit green and gold and the red-roofed town beneath them, tumbling to its silver sea. "I didn't know there were places like this," she said, and after another minute she added, "Once I had a dog . . ."

Gareth glanced at her.

". . . He would have loved it here."

"*She* can't stand dogs," said Gareth, and Binny, sensing that another great grumble about his father's girlfriend was about to begin, changed the subject.

"There's a tunnel," she said. "Look!"

It was a gorse tunnel. The bushes, that looked on top as

solid as enormous green and yellow-flowered hedgehogs, were hollow underneath. Except for the prickles it was quite easy to crawl through them. Binny set off to explore, and after a moment of hesitation Gareth followed her. Down there, the air was hot, sweet, and dusty with pollen, and the sunlight filtered through the bushes and painted runes and symbols on the ground. Binny and Gareth blinked when they broke through into a patch of sunshine. There the earth was thick with gorse needles, gray and brown against the bare ground.

"Look!" whispered Gareth.

Binny gazed, and it was as if the brown needles and the golden gritty earth had plaited themselves into a pattern. A thing alive. A supple curve and a small carved head. An eye like a crystal of dark fire. Then a rustle less than a leaf. A swift movement, and the patch of sunlight was empty again.

"What was it?" demanded Binny, amazed.

"It was an adder." Gareth sounded stunned. "An adder. I've never seen one. I've always looked, but I never have."

"Might it come back?"

"We could wait," said Gareth.

They waited, but it did not come back, and after a long time they gave up, crawled back out of their tunnel, and collected the bike.

"Why didn't I take a photograph?" mourned Gareth as they plodded home, taking turns to push, not bothering to ride.

"It doesn't matter. It's seeing it that counts. Only . . . Gareth?"

"What?"

"My mum and Clem are really, really scared of snakes. Even in a picture. I don't know what they'd say."

"I shall have to get my bike back in the shed without anyone seeing. I'm not supposed to be riding it this summer because of my arm."

Binny and Gareth looked at each other with perfect understanding. At that moment they were not enemies. They were friends, with a wonderful shared secret. Binny gave a small skip of pleasure. "Can you believe it?" she asked jubilantly, holding her hands wide apart. "It was so huge! And right there in front of us."

"What?" Gareth stopped walking and stared. Then he propped the bike on his hip to hold his hands a very different, much smaller distance apart. "It wasn't huge! It was this long! Max!"

"Just lying there, like a dragon!" continued Binny, taking no notice.

"Like a *dragon*!"

"For ages and ages!"

"Probably less than a minute."

"Tame as tame!"

"Tame!" repeated Gareth. "Are you crazy? Of course it wasn't tame!"

Binny, completely baffled, stared at him. "Gareth," she said. "I was there. I *saw* it! It was . . . it was . . ." She spread her hands helplessly. "And we watched it for hours before it slid away. Why are you pretending?"

"Me, pretending?" demanded Gareth with disbelief. "Me!"

They walked along in silence after that.

It was much easier for James to get along with Gareth. "Of course we're friends," he said.

"Why, *of course*?" asked Binny.

"Because"—James spoke with the deep, deep thankfulness of an only male in a feminine world—"he's a boy!"

"Just that?"

"And he knows all about trains, and he eats my lettuce."

James's lettuce was flourishing.

But is it poisonous? he wondered. Properly, thoroughly poisonous? Poisonous even when washed clean with shower gel? Poisonous on the inside? How would he ever know, when all of his family were so unhelpful? "No, thank you, James," they said when he offered his soapy little bunches.

"It's washed. It's lovely."

"You eat it, then."

Then Gareth came along.

"Dare you," said Binny, who happened to be around when James took him upstairs to admire his gardening skills, and she poked the seaside bucket containing the latest concoction (a dead crab, some tea bags, and a couple of banana skins) under the bed, out of sight.

"Why not?" asked Gareth, and he reached out of the window and picked himself a stalk.

"He didn't even wash it!" said James in admiration, but later, after Gareth had returned home, he poured the crab water away. Clearly it was not poisonous at all. Gareth had survived it far too well. James rescued the remains of the crab and pocketed it until he decided what to do with it. Then he prowled around the garden with his bucket.

There were a lot of dandelions.

"Dandelions, dandelions," sang James, gathering and squashing and stirring. "They make you wet the bed."

The dandelion water became a muddy green. James set it aside to grow magical, and turned to the crab.

"Must you bring that thing into the kitchen?" complained Clem.

"Yes, I must. It's ill."

"It's not ill, James," said his mother. "It's very very dead. Throw it away."

"I can't. I've got to have it for my farm. I've got hardly any animals so far."

"You've got all those sheep."

"Plastic."

"And the toad," said his mother.

"Still free-range," growled James.

"What about your snails?" asked Clem.

"I made them a field but they got over the walls."

"There's the chickens at the old ladies'," Binny reminded him. "Can't you pretend with them?"

"I'm not a pretend farmer," said James huffily, "and it's not fair that the old ladies have all those chickens and I don't have a single one."

"Old ladies aren't fair," said Binny. "Think of awful Aunty Violet!"

Binny's family groaned. Nobody wanted to think of awful Aunty Violet. As the summer progressed, as Clem's flute was heard more and more often, and as the worried look on the children's mother's face appeared less and less frequently, they were forgetting about awful Aunty Violet. In their minds she became a very different person. Perfectly-all-right Aunty Violet. Unusual, perhaps. Eccentric, even. Quick-tempered, possibly. Definitely reckless: all that smoking. Still, she had thought of them. They had the house. Their own front door, their own solid walls. James looked so well. The sea air was wonderful. It was so much what they had needed. It was going to work out. And, old and ill in Spain, she had planned it for them. She had even sent to Binny her particular regards.

Dear old Aunty Violet.

Not awful at all.

Don't be silly, Binny!

Aunty Violet, age sixteen, watched from her photo frame to see how Binny was taking this transformation. Binny marched upstairs with her, dumped her on the bathroom windowsill (with a direct view over the toilet), and took her troubles to Kate.

That was what everyone did, because Kate was interested in people. One day, when she had cleared enough tables and served enough coffees to finish paying her way through medical school, she would be a doctor, and everyone who knew her said she would be a very good one indeed. She was kind and she was clever, and she always, always listened.

She was stacking a dishwasher with thick white china when Binny arrived. The clatter was so loud that Binny had to shout.

"Kate!"

"If you'd like to earn yourself a milkshake, Bin, there's two sticky highchairs out the back need scrubbing."

"Are you very busy, Kate?"

"Sorry, Bin, you'll have to shout louder," said Kate, dealing plates like playing cards into the rack.

"ARE YOU VERY . . . oh, it doesn't matter."

Matter fell into a moment of silence between crashing crockery. Kate looked up for the first time and saw Binny's face.

"Of course it matters," she said, and took Binny to wash salad, a much quieter job.

"Tell me all your troubles," she ordered, and when Binny was silent, lost for how to begin, she added, "alphabetically. A?"

"Aunty Violet."

"B, Binny," said Kate. "C, Clem?"

"Not really, except . . ." Binny halted again.

"D, E, F?"

Binny shook her head.

"G? H, I, J?"

"James is all right."

"James is adorable," said Kate. "K? That could be me."

Binny rubbed her head affectionately against Kate's shoulder.

"L?"

"Liam," said Binny.

"What's he done?"

"Nothing."

"You still crew, then? No walking the plank or anything?"

"No. Has Liam got a girlfriend, Kate?"

"Girls on their vacations," said Kate. "That's the sort my brother likes. Fast turnover, no commitments, and they don't know his sister. He's got it all worked out!"

Binny smiled.

"Not L then," said Kate. "M?"

"Max," said Binny.

Most unexpectedly her eyes filled with tears. Worse, her nose became runny. Kate supplied her with paper towels, industrial-strength, and took her away from the lettuce.

"I need a private detective . . . Don't laugh, Kate!"

"I'm not laughing. Come outside, and we'll get on with those chairs. Now then. Go on."

"I used to have a dog. Max. Did Clem tell you?"

"*You* tell me."

"Max, and he was my dog, not everyone's, just mine."

"It never really works out like that with dogs and cats, though, does it?" remarked Kate mildly. "They don't seem to understand it, that they're not everyone's, I mean."

"Max did."

"Oh."

"Max knew he was mine, even after Dad died and he had to go and live with Granny. He still knew. Poor Max."

"Poor Binny," said Kate, and she handed Binny another square of paper towel.

"You haven't heard yet what Aunty Violet did."

"This is Aunty Violet who left you the house?"

"Yes, her. Who everybody thinks is lovely now. Except me."

"Right."

"She came back from Spain to visit Granny," said Binny, beginning to use the kitchen roll very vigorously, even though it was so stiff it hurt her nose. "To visit Granny. And Max was there. And we were in another town where one of Mum's friends said she could have a job."

"It's a pity you had to move away from Granny."

"Yes, it was. I wanted to stay with her, but they wouldn't let me. Granny was very old."

"Oh dear," murmured Kate.

"So anyway, while we were all miles away and didn't know anything about it, Aunty Violet visited Granny. And she met Max. She was horrible about Max. She said he was terror . . . terrorizing Granny!"

"Terrorizing?"

"'Course he wasn't. He was still only very young. Not even one."

"Bouncy, probably," suggested Kate.

"Yes. Just bouncy. All puppies jump about and bark and bite a bit. Everyone knows that."

"Pass me that sponge, Binny, and tell me what Aunty Violet did and why you need a private detective."

"She got rid of Max."

"Without telling you?"

"Yes. Granny told us ages later, when Aunty Violet'd gone back to Spain."

Kate shook her head to indicate sorrow. "Did you ever ask her where Max went?"

"Yes, I did, at Granny's funeral, just before she died."

"Granny had her funeral just before she died?"

"No, no! Just before Aunty Violet died! Granny was dead already and it was her funeral and it was snowy and Clem fainted so there was just Aunty Violet and me in the car."

"This is a terrible story," remarked Kate. "Tragedy upon tragedy. Go on. You asked Aunty Violet and Aunty Violet wouldn't tell you?"

"How do you know that?"

"And she wouldn't tell you because she knew if she did you'd give no peace to anyone until you found him again? Just guessing."

Binny nodded.

"How long ago was all this?"

"Last winter was Granny's funeral, in all that snow. But it's more than two years since Aunty Violet got rid of Max."

Kate said very gently, "Don't you think Max will have found a new life in more than two years, Binny?"

"No."

"I don't know, but I'm guessing private detectives cost a fortune."

"A quarter of the house is mine. That would be enough."

"But you would have to sell it," said Kate. "Sell the house, where you are all so happy."

"We could buy another, with the leftover money. Smaller."

"Not much smaller," said Kate thoughtfully, "or else your poor Mum would probably end up sleeping in the street."

Binny gave a small grin.

"You've done so well, Binny," said Kate. "You've managed without Max all this time."

"Not really, I haven't."

"You've managed since I've known you. Happy enough. Now, do you want to know what I would do if I were you?"

"What?"

"I'd start writing letters. People take notice of letters. Phone calls vanish. E-mails disappear when you turn off the screen. But letters are real. They have a shape. They stay around. So if I were you, I'd begin writing them."

"Who to?"

"All the RSPCA branches in the town where Granny lived. All the vets. All the rescue places and animal shelters."

"He won't be in those places now, though, Kate."

"No, but somebody might be who remembers him. You could try anyway. You can be your own private detective!"

Binny suddenly smiled a real smile.

"Thank you, Kate!"

"Hop off and clear some tables for me. You need to start saving up for stamps."

"It's a *brilliant* idea!" said Binny, and two minutes later had forgotten she had ever been in need of industrial-strength paper towels and was racing around outside, swishing bubbles over the tables and stacking turrets of glass and china.

"Drop that lot and we're bankrupt," remarked Liam, visiting between seal trips to scrounge a free coffee. "Hang on, I'll get the door. Coming out with me when we go again?"

"She's doing the tables first," said Kate, overhearing.

"Whose crew is she, mine or yours?" demanded Liam. "You've already grabbed Clem! You leave Binny to me! Hurry up out here, Bin, and come down to the harbor. There's a pound coin under that menu, by the way! I'll have it if you don't need it!"

"I do! I do! I need stamps!" said Binny, dumped her tray, grabbed the coin, hugged Kate, and hurried after Liam, running to keep up.

Happy, thought Kate, smiling after her.

Or happy enough.

Chapter Twelve

"That Gareth comes round nearly every day now," remarked Clem one morning as she and Binny washed the breakfast things together. "Over the fence and straight into the house like he owns it."

"I know," agreed Binny, "and then he stares around like a visitor at a zoo or something."

"He's very polite," said Clem. "Too polite."

"Only to you. But he's nice to James. He eats his lettuce."

"I know. Did the dandelions work?"

"Hope so," said Binny.

They both laughed callously.

"What did he water it with this morning?" asked Clem.

"Old sneaker soup from the old sneaker he found on the beach. He soaked it in bath water and strained off the juice."

"You should warn Gareth, Binny. That's the worst yet."

"Mmm," said Binny. She had no intention of warning

Gareth. He had not warned her the day before when he had given her a chili to munch. Besides, what use was an enemy that you had to look out for? She and Gareth had been excellent enemies since their trip to the gorse moor. Perhaps because they had shared a secret. And perhaps also because they had both realized how very differently they each saw things. (Binny's long look at a huge tame dragon. Gareth's glimpse of a small wild adder.) Somehow they were bound even closer by mutual misunderstanding.

It led to a lot of testing.

Every day there was something new. Gareth had kindly loaned Binny his giant water squirter, and encouraged her to lie down on her back and fire it up the chimney.

"It'll clean it, you see," he explained, and added, having begun to understand the state of the family's finances, "That will save you having to pay someone to come!"

Gareth's method had cleaned the chimney beautifully, mostly all over Binny, who had had to be hosed down in the garden. It took three washes to get the soot out of her hair and because of this, before she handed the water squirter back, she had topped up its reservoir with duck-egg blue paint.

"Did it work, then?" asked Gareth, as innocently as if he had not witnessed the hosing in the garden.

"Not very well. I thought it would be more powerful, being so big."

"More powerful?" asked Gareth indignantly. "It's only the biggest you can buy!"

"Well, it doesn't seem to work very well when you fire it straight up," said Binny, and prudently retired to the shelter of the apple tree while Gareth pumped the water squirter to exploding point, fired it upward, and turned duck-egg blue.

No one except Binny witnessed this pleasant event (although it was very obvious to Gareth's family that something catastrophic had occurred on their patio). Binny's family knew nothing about it at all, which was why Clem asked, "Why don't you ever go to Gareth's house instead of him always coming here?"

"I don't want to, that's why," said Binny. The patio had scrubbed clean quite well, but there was also the day of the helicopter flight on her conscience.

"James doesn't ever go there either."

"That's because he's mad at them because they called him a girl."

"They did?"

"She did. A *little* girl! Poor James!"

"I suppose he was wearing that wetsuit? What happened then?"

"You remember Mum sent him into the garden to be out of the way while we cleared up all the soot and water?"

"Go on."

"And it was a really hot afternoon?"

"What's that got to do with anything?"

"Really hot and quiet and James heard pigs."

"Pigs?"

"Through the fence. So he climbed up the apple tree to look because he couldn't see over. He said he thought if wild pigs had come to live in Gareth's garden, he would make a hole in the fence and get them for his farm. But when he got up the tree, it wasn't pigs. It was Gareth's father, snoring, right under our apple tree on one of those posh stripy sunbed things."

Clem, who had finished washing the dishes, found a tea towel and began to help dry.

"Thanks," said Binny gratefully and dropped a mug.

"Binny!"

"Shall I keep telling you about James?"

"Yes. But quickly! Gareth's father snoring. No pigs. Hurry up!"

"Yes. And you know how little hard apples fall off our apple tree if you joggle the branches a bit? Well, they did. An apple fell straight into Gareth's father's wide-open mouth!"

"Binny! He could have choked!"

"He did choke, and he rolled around with his eyes all bulgy and then Gareth, who must have been watching, ran out of the house and tipped him off the posh sunbed thing and hit him really hard on his back and the apple shot out and James laughed so much he slipped out of the tree onto those frilly pink flowers they've got growing round the edge of their grass. And, she must have seen James fall because she came rushing out of the house too, and she said, 'Gareth, Gareth, is the little girl hurt?'"

"What about Gareth's father being hurt?" demanded Clem.

"Oh, he was all right. But James was really annoyed. Do you think we should get his hair cut?"

"What?"

"Do you think we should get James's hair cut so he doesn't look so much like a girl?" asked Binny. "Why are you staring?"

"Am I staring?" asked Clem. "I'm sorry. I must learn to take you more casually."

"So anyway, that's why James doesn't go round to Gareth's. Nothing to do with the fence. They didn't notice. It was hardly scorched."

But Clem had gone. With her hands over her ears. Begging,

"Don't tell me about the fence, don't tell me about the fence!"

"Weird," said Binny.

They had to keep making new rules for James.

No taking money from the old ladies.

No hunting in trash cans.

No taking off that wetsuit in shops to show people you are a boy.

No more stealing lettuce seeds from the supermarket.

In fact no more stealing anything from the supermarket.

No crabs in your bedroom.

Or Binny's bedroom.

No tormenting the neighbors.

No matches. No unsupervised hotness of any kind.

"He's only six," said Clem, because it seemed such a long list for a very small boy.

Because he was only six, they (most confusingly, no wonder he hardly ever knew right from wrong) tolerated:

Wearing the things he found in trash cans.

Growing the stolen lettuce seeds.

Trying to make the lettuce grow poisonous.

Testing it on Gareth.

The crab in the kitchen if he kept the lid on the box.

Sucking his fingers when telling lies.

Occasional record-breaking attempts on the garden fence.

"But only sometimes," they added sternly, splash marks on the fence ranking in all their minds far worse than poisoning the neighbors with stolen property.

"Sometimes," agreed James, amiably accepting this madness.

"Not all the time."

"For a treat," said James, contentedly sucking his fingers.

"But *why*?"

James could not say why. He had no idea of the reason for half the things he did. Sometimes it was as if the fence whispered *"Find a match!" "Taste me!"* ordered hard green apples, seaweed, soap, and cobwebs. *"How awful would it be,"* questioned the house key, foolishly given to James to hold on a family trip to watch the sunset over the sea, *"if you dropped me in the harbor?"* James looked at the cold reflecting water, knew it would be truly awful, and dropped the key.

The old ladies at the old people's home said:

Little devil.

Take no notice, my lovely!

He's got it all worked out.

Butter wouldn't melt.

It doesn't mean a thing at his age.

They understood him down to his bones.

The combined ages of all the old ladies in the home came to almost four thousand years. Almost four thousand years of undemanding tolerance bathed around James like sunshine whenever he appeared. No wonder his eyes sparkled when he stepped through the door.

"I'm getting chickens," he told the old ladies, and they did not argue as his family would have done. They said, "I thought you young ones were all into computer games these days," and "Chickens. Well."

Some of them were actual chicken experts and gave him mysterious, chicken-flavored advice.

"You don't want a rooster."

"Turn them over twice and you can fold them up like a package."

"They'll bring in the foxes."

"They'll clean up your snails."

James's toes curled with excitement as he absorbed this information. At night in his bedroom he replayed the words again in his head. Turn them over twice? But how? And over what? Surely a rooster would be magnificent? Exactly how would a chicken set about cleaning a snail? Like Kate's cat cleaned her kittens? Would they really bring in the foxes? Where would a chicken get a fox? Did the chickens at the old people's home bring in foxes?

"Not yet, but they will," said the old ladies.

"How much do chickens cost?" he asked his most chicken-wise old lady.

"A mort."

"A *what*?"

"I told you."

A mort, thought James, and something pounded warm in his chest because he had never heard a more satisfying word. He pondered a mort for a day and a night.

"A lot of money," he whispered. "It must be. A mort."

However, he was not discouraged. He remembered Clem and her flute lessons. He knew how money was acquired.

First of all, you needed stuff.

Valuable stuff.

Already he had the warm red stone and Ella's watch that was an insult and that he had been told to put out of sight.

That was a start.

Ancient Mrs. Innes could not wear her rings. They slipped away from her thin white fingers. She kept them instead in an old Dutch shoe, along with small coins, buttons, and paper clips.

"Are those rubies?"

"No, just garnets."

"Is that gold?"

"It had better be."

"If they won't stay on your fingers . . . Mrs. Innes, Mrs. Innes . . . wake up and listen! If they won't stay on your fingers you could wear them on your thumbs!"

"Ha!" said Mrs. Innes, blinking. Her laughter was a thin, ringing sound like the echo inside a seashell. "Wear them on your own thumbs!"

"Wouldn't you . . . Mrs. Innes, you've shut your eyes again! Wouldn't you mind?"

"I'm done minding. Off you go and shut the door."

He was like a little magpie. He put the rings in the box that had once held his snails, along with the watch and the warm red stone. After that he put the box far back in the darkness under his bed. Sometimes he forgot it and sometimes he remembered. Then he would fish it out and ponder its contents. He wondered and wondered how close he was to a mort.

The Rock Pools IV

"How do you feel?"

Gareth opened his eyes. He peered at his arm, and at Binny's red fingers and the blood-soaked wedge of sock. He took a while to answer. "Bit floaty," he mumbled at last.

Binny sacrificed her other sock to tie the first in place. By this time there was blood everywhere. Even Gareth's glasses were smeared and each of Binny's fingernails was a dark crimson curve. She abandoned Gareth for a minute to slosh her hands in a breaking wave.

"Good thing there aren't sharks" she called, which caused Gareth to rouse up.

"'Course there's sharks," he said.

"WHAT?"

"Loads of them!"

"Gareth! Proper sharks? Big sharks? The sort that smell blood?"

"They all smell blood," said Gareth.

Binny scrambled hastily back up the rock. "Hadn't we better

go now?" she asked anxiously. "I'm going to roll the net up so all those hooks are safe in the middle. Then do you think you can help carry it?"

Gareth managed carrying more easily than he expected, better than Binny, who with one eye continually on the horizon looking for triangular fins, kept stumbling into rocks. It took a long time to make their way over and between the jumbled granite of the headland back to the level stretch where the rock pools began. "And we've still all that slippery black stuff to get across," said Binny as they rounded the last rocky outcrop.

Then she stopped.

There was no slippery black stuff. There were no rock pools. There was just a churning whiteness. The headland, that rocky height, was now an island.

The sun was still high and bright, but Binny shivered, then, to cover up the shiver, said bravely, "It c-c-can't be all that deep."

Gareth, who had also been taking in the scene as well as he could through the remains of his glasses, said calmly, "It won't even be up to our knees."

"N-n-no."

"Anyway, I got my thousand meters! Swimming," he added, when Binny did not respond. "Can you?"

Could she?

Binny remembered the last day of term. The wonderful

astonishment of the school swimming prize! Would they have given her that prize if she could not swim? Certainly not!

"Of course!" said Binny, and stepped into the water.

After all, it was only ankle-deep. And perhaps at most a hundred meters across, estimated Gareth (the thousand-meter swimmer). But icy. Bone-aching. Much colder than the waves that had broken over them earlier.

"Why's it so c-c-cold?" she asked Gareth, taking a second awful step.

"Because it's fresh from the Atlantic and there's icebergs in it farther north," said Gareth, and stepped firmly forward. "Come on! It's okay. I can manage the net."

"You can't."

Gareth, to prove that he could, hitched the whole bundle onto his left shoulder, and stepped farther into the water. Still less than knee-deep. He took a couple more steps, decided it was easy, and turned to see how Binny was doing.

She seemed to have come to a halt.

"I'm just waiting till I get used to it," she said defensively.

"Move!" commanded Gareth.

"I will."

"Quickly."

"I can't."

"Dare you."

Binny gave him a look of anguish, plunged forward, lost her footing, and was suddenly waist-deep. She gasped, staggered, and did some of her prize-winning swimming.

"Grab hold of the net!" said Gareth, and she grabbed, found her footing, and arrived beside him totally drenched.

"What on earth did you do that for?" he demanded.

"I didn't do it on p-p-purpose!" said Binny, shivering and indignant. "It was a rock pool! I stepped right into an invisible rock pool! I don't think we can do this."

"We have to."

Gareth started forward again, and still his steps held, solid rock beneath his feet. "Follow me!" he commanded Binny, and a moment later was hit by an incoming wave. It caught the back of his knees so hard that he sat down neck-deep in his own invisible rock pool. Binny, lurching to the rescue, dragged him upright again.

"Do you have to keep bleeding into the water?" she complained.

"Yes." Gareth waited until the latest wave swept past them. "Come on!"

This time he disappeared completely. White bubbles foamed where he had been and the net swirled loosely amongst them. Binny gathered it with difficulty, whimpering a little, until his head rose up in front of her, and then the rest of him swam into view and she heard his usual staccato curses: Soaked, Hell, Rubbish, *and knew he was all right.*

"*Back,*" *he gasped.*

Step by step, clutching each other, the net, and accidental hand-fuls of salt water, they made their way back to their starting point. Gareth's glasses were gone, and now he was in a world like an Impressionist painting, swirling liquid colors, where the outlines mingled and were lost. So only Binny saw the danger that was approaching: an enormous, bulging muscle of green ocean, head height, clear as glass. They reached the rocks at the moment it broke and Binny just had time to screech, "Hold on!" before it erupted over them.

Chapter Thirteen

Every day Aunty Violet's house became more of a home. They learned its ways. How to manage the shower so they did not alternately scald and freeze. Which windows jammed and which fell open. With a borrowed hammer and a handful of nails they cured the hideous creak on the stairs, eliminating at the same time at least one of Aunty Violet's ghosts.

Outside, the jungle, although not exactly tamed, was pushed back enough to allow room for a picnic table, a path to the apple tree, and a patch of dry scratchy grass where James laid out his farm. Inside, Clem and her mother and quite often Kate as well, continued to paint. They were on to the bedrooms now. Yellow for Binny (which made Clem groan) and blue for James. James's walls looked very bare until Kate arrived and added white clouds and sunshine.

"And seagulls?" asked James, remembering the paintings on the café walls.

Kate could paint gulls very quickly. A flicker of black and white for wings, a few dabs of Binny's yellow for beaks, and they appeared in flocks, swooping across the blue-sky walls.

Binny looked at them in admiration.

"Could you do dogs?"

"Sorry, Binny, I can only do birds," said Kate.

"Could *you* do dogs?" Binny asked Liam (who had arrived for five minutes and stayed more than two hours).

"Dogs?" repeated Liam, as if dogs were exotic creatures he had never yet encountered.

"Yes. You know, black and white ones. Like seagulls."

"Nope," said Liam. "Black and white dogs like seagulls, definitely not. Are you and Clem off back to work, then, Kate? I'll walk down with you if you are."

"Seals, then," suggested Binny, as they all set off five minutes later. "Could you, Liam? On my bedroom walls?"

"Haven't you seen enough seals?" demanded Liam. "I know I have. Crikey, look down there at the harbor. I've got a line waiting! Bye, Clem, Kate! Come on, Bin, if you're coming! Don't let them escape!"

Binny ran so fast, that Liam rewarded her with the rare and honorable job of untying the last holding rope from its bollard. "Well done!" he said, as she jumped the widening gap between steps and boat as if she'd been doing it for years. "Put on that life jacket and go and sit with those boys," he added, looking over his boatload of passengers. "They look like trouble! Tell them to get their hands out of the water. Tell them you're crew!"

Binny made her way toward the boys as Liam steered out of the harbor. The first of them, who looked about her age, slyly stuck out a leg and tripped her as she passed.

"You did that on purpose!" said Binny. "And you're to take your hands out of the water!"

"Do you own this boat or something?" one of them asked.

"No, she owns the sea," said another, and they heaved with laughter.

"Actually I'm crew," said Binny with dignity. "So you're to do what I say."

"As if!" the one who had tripped her sniggered.

"You're not crew," said another, contemptuously.

"Show them your jacket, Bin," suddenly bellowed Liam from the front of the boat, "and let me know if we're going to have to turn back!"

That sobered the boys. They looked at Liam, and they read the back of Binny's jacket, and they took their hands out of the water and began complaining instead.

"Why doesn't everyone have a life jacket?" one of them asked.

"You can if you want," said Binny. "They're in that big box in the middle. Help yourself."

"Are there any more with *crew* written on?"

"Of course not."

"I don't want one, then. Are we nearly there?"

"Yes. Look."

Having failed to find the seals at their handiest location just across the bay, Liam had turned toward the little island. Now he was slowing down, because they had been successful. A couple of seals were sprawled on the rocky beach, and when Liam cut the engine and the noise of it died away, round shining heads began appearing all about the boat. People began to point with excitement and take photographs, and Binny went forward to collect the mackerel bucket.

"She really is crew," Binny heard one boy say to another as she began tossing chunks of fish to the seals. On the way home they behaved quite differently, respectfully shuffling their legs out of the way when Binny stepped past.

"You are lucky," said one of them enviously, when they were once more tied up by the harbor wall, and everyone was lining up to climb out. "Will you be going back there again today?"

"Depends," said Binny, swirling water around in the bucket to rinse out the slime. "We don't always go the same way."

"How do you know where the seals will be?"

"Oh," said Binny, leaning with nautical recklessness to wash her fishy hands over the side of the boat. "'S'perience, I suppose. Can I get past you to reach my mop?"

The boy stepped aside and watched while Binny dipped and swished.

"I guess you have to know all about seals and steering and that?" he asked.

"Oh yes. Yes, you do."

"And lifesaving and first aid and currents and tides?"

Binny was rescued from being forced to admit to these talents by Liam calling, "Come up here, Bin, and get your photograph taken!"

For the boys' benefit, Binny rolled her eyes skyward, as if having her photograph taken as part of Liam's crew was an all-too-familiar chore. Inside, however, her heart bumped with pride as she scurried up the steps. She felt very nearly famous as she posed with her mop. Liam laughed at the wideness of her smile.

"If your friends could see you now!" he teased.

"Yes," agreed Binny, and privately she thought, *or even better, my enemies!*

Gareth.

Gareth, the always scornful. She wished he could have heard those boys. *You are lucky!* and *She really is crew!*

"Liam, if I brought somebody with me, would they have to pay?"

"Who? James? Clem?"

"No, no. You saw him before. That boy."

"The one who came racing down and jumped the harbor corner with you and then sloped off?"

"Yes."

"Of course he'd have to pay. The usual. Four fifty."

"Oh, Liam!"

"You can bring Clem for free if you like. Or James and your mum. Not James without your mum!"

"But that's not fair, Liam! Just because Mum and Clem and James are nice!"

"This boy you want to bring isn't nice? Why'd you want to bring not-nice people on my boat, Bin?"

Binny didn't reply. She was examining her pockets for money. Only the day before she had had nearly four pounds, but Kate had found her a list of Max addresses on the Internet. Binny had taken it up into the apple tree and spent two agonizing hours writing six pleading letters. A lot of her money had gone on stamps.

"Okay, okay! I didn't realize you were paying," said Liam at last, after several minutes of torture watching Binny count out pennies and five pences. "He can come half-price and I hope he enjoys it. He looks the sort who gets seasick to me!"

Even at half price, the cost of the ticket for Gareth was beyond Binny at that moment. She spent the rest of the day clearing tables for Kate and treasure hunting under plates and saucers.

"Got it!" she said at last, and went home very pleased with herself.

James was also very pleased with himself. He had spent the afternoon on the beach, where he too had found treasure. He displayed it proudly to his mother and sisters: a large yellow skull.

"A sheep," said James. "Fallen off the cliffs. Drowned in the sea. Eaten up by fishes. Washed up on the beach. For my farm."

He cradled it lovingly. "There was its eyes. There was its nose. There was its teeth before they fell out. Will Aunty Violet be a skull by now?"

"James!"

"How long does it take? Will—"

"James, have you watered your lettuce today?" interrupted Clem. "There's some awful-smelling milk in the kitchen if you haven't!"

"Really awful?"

"Deadly."

James tucked his skull up under a cushion and hurried off to mix deadly milk with sneaker juice and pour it out of his bedroom window. Clem and her mother went into the kitchen and began a sort of alchemy that would turn eggs and potatoes into thick golden tortillas. Binny looked at Aunty Violet, age sixteen, thought of her skull, took her from her latest place on the bookshelf (where she had been put so that she could watch television instead of unnerving her relations in the bathroom), and stuffed her away under the telephone.

The moment she had done it, the telephone rang, and Binny was seized with a brand-new fear, a possibility of horror that she had not considered before.

It rang again. It was an old phone that had been in the house when they arrived. Once Aunty Violet must have answered it. Once her hand had held it. Once her voice had spoken. As clearly as if she was in the room Binny heard that voice again. *Binny, listen to me!*

For a third time the phone rang. Hard and insistent.

Binny backed away until she reached the door, pulled it open, and fell sobbing into the kitchen.

"What on earth . . . ?" began her mother. "Binny! Clem, for goodness sake, answer that phone!"

"NO!" cried Binny. "Don't answer it! Don't answer it!" and she fled wailing through the kitchen into the garden and then up into the kindly arms of the apple tree.

"Binny, darling, please come down."

"No."

"Binny, what a fuss about nothing! Do you know, it was only Kate for Clem?"

"Yes, but it might not have been."

"Binny, please tell me what frightened you so much!"

"I can't."

"Would you talk to Clem or Kate?"

"No, I wouldn't! Leave me alone!"

In the end they did leave her alone, or nearly alone. Not quite, because James, in his pink and green wetsuit, unexpectedly appeared and stationed himself at the bottom of the tree.

"Go away," said Binny ungratefully.

"I'm on guard," he explained, "in case you fall out in one of your states."

"What use would you be if I did?"

"I've brought cushions."

"What?"

"Cushions," repeated James. "Look!"

Binny looked, and sure enough, there were the two green cushions from the sofa, carefully placed at the foot of the tree. They looked so inadequate, and James looked so pleased with himself as he stood beside them, that she could not help a small smile.

"Oh, James!"

"Are you getting better?"

"Yes."

"A lot or a bit?"

"A bit, anyway."

"Are you coming down, then?"

"I think I'd rather stay here."

"Stay!" agreed James magnificently.

"Perhaps forever!"

"Or until you need the toilet," said James, with tactless practicality.

"What!"

James looked at his two sofa cushions.

"I might have to move them," Binny heard him murmur slightly anxiously, and the last of her fear left her as she melted into laughter.

*   *   *

"She's still up the tree," reported James, passing through the kitchen to collect his skull and his toothbrush, "but she's not in a state!"

Binny stayed in the apple tree for so long that at suppertime her mother climbed up with her plate.

"This is my favorite place in the world," Binny told her.

"Lucky you to have your favorite place in the world so close to home!"

"Could I sleep here, do you think?"

"Well. Perhaps. One day."

"One day in real life, or one day like when James gets his chickens?"

"One day when you've made it a bit safer. It's quite wobbly, isn't it?"

"I could tie myself on."

"I'll keep thinking about that one, Binny," said her mother, and climbed back down again.

The sounds of the evening came filtering through the silver-green leaves to Binny. She heard Gareth's family light a barbecue and Gareth announce that he was not hungry.

"Tell me why we bother!" she heard a voice cry, and then the barbecue smoke drifted away.

She heard seagulls, footsteps on the cobbled street, James washing dishes in a bowl on the picnic table (he was still young enough to consider washing dishes a treat), and her mother reading aloud to him as he splashed. James and she had joined the library.

"Binny!" called their mother. "Binny, I meant to tell you! You know that how-to-tame-your-dragon book you read just before we came away?"

"Yes?"

"There's a whole row of them in the library. We looked, just in case."

"A whole row? Why didn't you get me one?"

"We thought you might like to do it yourself."

"Anyway we couldn't," called James from his dishes. "You can only get six books at a time and there's more than six books about chickens."

"You got six books about chickens?"

"Yes, 'cos there wasn't none about poison. Not in the children's part. Not that we could see."

"You could have got one dragon book."

"Go yourself, tomorrow."

"I won't have time. I'll be out with Liam."

"Are you still wearing that life jacket, Binny?" asked her mother.

"I have to, so people know I'm crew," said Binny. "A lady took my photograph today. With Liam and her little girl. Standing beside the boat."

"Famous," said her mother.

"I'm famous," remarked James, wet from the neck down from washing dishes. "Wherever I go, people know it's me."

"The boy in the girl's wetsuit," said Clem.

"Soon to become the boy in bed," said their mother. "Come on, quickly, James! Early start tomorrow, if you're coming to work with me."

James went inside quite happily. They could put him to bed, but they couldn't make him sleep. Bath, bed, story. *Good night, then, James! Good night, don't kiss me,* and out he would hop in his pajamas to watch the street from his window. There was the three-legged cat. There was a big boy, eating chips. There was Gareth's father, cross-faced as usual. There was an old lady who looked like Aunty Violet, except she's dead, thought James, remembering his skull, so she won't look like that. There was his lettuce, wonderfully green. He looked at it thoughtfully and calculated angles. His bed was a cabin bed, which put him up quite high. Would he, or would he not, fall out of the window?

There was Clem and that was probably her boyfriend . . .
James slid down from his lookout perch and into his bed.

"Hey! Gareth! Can you hear me! I've got a surprise!"

Binny was awake early and calling out of her window. After
five minutes or so, Gareth's grumpy, smeary-spectacled morning face appeared.

"What do you want?"

"I've got you a present!"

"Why?" asked Gareth, suspicious at once.

"Because . . . because . . ." Binny hunted around for a
good reason to give Gareth a present. "It's something to say
sorry because I was so rude to your dad!"

Gareth stared.

"I don't mind you being rude to my dad," he said, sound-
ing completely surprised. "Go ahead! Feel free! I do it all
the time!"

"Still, I really am sorry and I did get you a present."

"I might not want it. And I hope you don't think I'm
going to give you one back."

"It's a free trip on the seal boat!" said Binny, ignoring
these ungracious remarks. "This afternoon. You'll love it!
Everyone does. And you'll be able to see me being crew. I
paid for it with my table-clearing money."

"Well, you can unpay, then," said Gareth ungratefully. "I'm not going. I've told you a million times."

"You haven't."

"I hate boats and they make me sick."

"Not this one won't," said Binny, although she couldn't help remembering Liam's opinion on that subject. "It's not that sort of boat."

"They're all that sort of boat!"

"I've been going out on it for ages and ages. Nearly all summer, and nobody's ever been sick."

"Yet," said Gareth. "Anyway, I'm doing something else today. So sorry. Can't go."

"What are you doing?"

"Mind your own!"

"Nothing, I bet. Sulking, as usual. Like you did when they lit that barbecue last night."

"What do you know about that?"

"I heard."

"I just didn't feel like eating his rotten burnt black muck," said Gareth, "or her rubbishy salad. I felt like cereal. What's wrong with that? And as a matter of fact, not that it's anything to do with you, today I'm going out on my bike."

"Where are you going?"

"Along the cliff path to where the rock pools are."

"There's rock pools everywhere," objected Binny.

"Not like where I'm going. There's a hundred."

"A hundred?"

"Yes. It's famous. People have counted. And it's miles away from this dump and miles away from them. So double good."

"I'll come with you," said Binny.

"You won't."

"I will. We can share your bike like we did before. I'll come with you to the rock pools (I don't believe there's a hundred, though) and then this afternoon you can come with me to the seals."

"I've told you. I'm not going on that boat."

"Oh, Gareth."

"I'm just not."

"I thought you'd love it."

"What a lie!"

Binny lowered her eyes, looked away, took a deep breath.

"Oh no, oh no, oh no you don't!" yelled Gareth, grabbing at the window frame and pulling it shut so hastily that he trapped his own head.

"Dare you."

"You are so . . . so . . . predictable!" howled Gareth, extracting his ears, but losing his glasses.

"Let's take food, and have it at the rock pools."

"I'm not packing up a stupid picnic."

"I will, then. We've got a whole cold pizza that nobody wanted last night. And bananas and things! Lots of things! Come round for me when you're ready!"

"Oh, all right," said Gareth.

"Gareth and me are going out along the cliff path," Binny told her family at breakfast time. "To a place where he says there's a hundred rock pools but I don't believe him. Is that all right?"

"To not believe him or to go?" asked Clem.

"It's all right as long as Gareth has his cell phone and you stay together," said her mother. "And no swimming. James, don't eat orange peel. It will give you a stomachache."

"Is it poisonous?" asked James hopefully.

"Hardly."

"If you had one hardly poisonous thing like orange peel and you mixed it up with another hardly poisonous thing like . . . like . . ."

"Salt?" suggested Clem.

"Is salt poisonous?"

"Depends how much you eat."

"Well, do they add up and make extra strong poisonous?"

"Mmm," said his family. "Try it and see."

★ ★ ★

James was at the bottom of the garden, pounding orange peel between two stones, when Gareth appeared.

"Gareth!" he said.

"Yes?"

"Go round the back of the apple tree and look at the fence."

Gareth did, and came back with his eyebrows raised high.

"Pretty good!"

James's eyes sparkled up at him for a moment before he dropped his head and went back to his pounding.

"What are you mixing with that orange peel?" asked Gareth curiously.

"Sugar."

"Why sugar?"

"To be like salt. I couldn't find the salt."

Gareth looked down at James, so hopeful, so close to marmalade, and he felt more kindly toward him than he had to any human being all summer.

"Need any help?" he asked.

"Not now," said James. "One day, perhaps."

"Anytime," said Gareth.

Binny and Gareth, sharing the bike, passed the journey to the rock pools in a series of silent dares.

It was not a good path for a bike, narrow, and crumbling into unexpected hollows. Every now and then it would swoop perilously down toward the cliff edge so that nothing but good luck and a strand or two of rusty wire separated the rider from the brink. Binny and Gareth took pride in crossing these horrible places at top speed, and at times it was very hard for the one watching the cyclist not to shriek. Once Binny did, and Gareth for a brief and frightening moment turned, smirked in triumph, and raised both arms into the air. When Binny tried to do the same she lost her balance completely. The bike skidded from under her and came to rest with the back wheel hanging over the cliff and spinning busily in space. Binny landed a meter or two ahead, vanishing entirely in a scratchy patch of heather.

Gareth, who had seen the beginning of the skid but not the end, shouted out in fear.

"I'm here!" called Binny from her heather.

Gareth stopped panicking very abruptly and concentrated on looking for damage on his bike.

"I'm surprised the chain's not off," he grumbled.

"Don't you care that I nearly slid over the cliff?"

"I'm glad my bike didn't. What's so funny?"

"You are."

Gareth looked at her suspiciously, seeing nothing to laugh at.

"Anyway, we're there," he said. "This is it. Come on."

Huge granite slabs, like the tumbled steps of giants, led down to a rocky headland. Binny recognized it as the place Liam sometimes visited as a last resort, when the seals could not be found nearer home. All amongst the granite slabs were rock pools. Bright green ones that the sea hardly visited except at the highest of tides. Sparkling pink and silver ones on the edge of the waves. Gareth dipped and lingered between them like a rock pool reader in a rock pool bookshop. Binny started to count, gave up, and stretched out on the warm stone to watch the sky.

"Did you really bring pizza?" called Gareth after a while.

"Yes. Pepperoni."

Binny retrieved her backpack and began pulling things out. Flattened pizza, squashed bananas, and crumbly ginger cream cookies.

"I rolled right over when I fell," she said regretfully.

"Doesn't matter," said Gareth, chewing already. "Loads better than *Her* cooking."

"I think," remarked Binny, "that you are the sort of person who hates a lot of people. There's two sorts of people. One sort likes people until something makes them hate them. And the other sort hates people until something makes them like them. And you're the second sort."

"Yes, I am," agreed Gareth, reaching for the bananas.

"Finish the pizza if you like."

Gareth finished the pizza, three bananas, and most of the cookies and flopped backward, stuffed. Binny, with her chin on her arms, gazed dreamily out to sea. "Soon that's where we'll be," she remarked.

Gareth sat up very suddenly.

"You forgot!" said Binny.

Gareth did not reply.

"I don't know why you're so scared," said Binny. "Babies go on the seal boat. *Old ladies* go!"

Gareth took off his glasses and fumbled to wipe them on the front of his shirt. His shoulders twitched. Binny felt sorry for him.

"Anyway," she told him comfortingly, "I'll be there. Crew!" she could not resist adding.

"Is that supposed to make me feel better?"

"Doesn't it?"

"No."

The journey back was less cheerful than the journey there. They still took turns, but they were not fair turns.

Gareth left Binny all the uphill parts and all the places where the path turned suddenly toward the edge of the cliff. His mood grew blacker and blacker.

"Oh, all right," Binny said at last. "You don't have to come. I'll let you off."

"Too late," said Gareth sullenly. "A dare's a dare. You can't let me off."

Still, it was lovely at the harbor, with the crowds and the gulls and Liam giving out orders. "Hurry up! What are you doing with that bike? You can't leave it there without a lock! Somebody will have it the minute we leave! Get a move on, Binny, and take it across to Kate! Tell her to put it round the back. And run!"

Binny seized the bike and ran. Gareth looked at the boat in disgust, shrugged, and grimly climbed down to his fate. He sat apart from everyone else, feeling self-conscious and awkward. Binny seemed to be gone for a very long time, and when she reappeared, panting and pink-faced, she was seized at once by Liam.

"Where on earth have you been? Never mind, never mind! Hop down to the boat! There's fourteen Brownies all needing life jackets! Can you go and sort them out?"

Binny beamed. Fourteen Brownies, she knew, were a

wonderful catch. A boatload, by the time their leaders were packed on board. A well-behaved boatload too.

The little Brownies lined up politely for their life jackets, took what was handed out to them with no complaints, murmured their thanks, sat down exactly where Binny ordered, and tucked their legs neatly out of her way. Their leaders were equally charming, accepting with hardly a murmur of protest Liam's No Discount for Group Parties rule. "Now, where do you want us?" they asked Binny, and Binny, glowing with pride and importance, stowed them away. Now and then, she glanced across at Gareth to see if he was noticing this new, nautical, responsible version of herself.

"Did you manage all right without me this morning?" she dared to ask Liam, and he, wonderfully, instead of being sarcastic, shouted above the roar of the newly started engine, "Oh well. I struggled through!"

"Do you want a life jacket?" Binny asked, sitting down beside Gareth.

"No, thanks, I'd rather drown," answered Gareth promptly. "I'd *much* rather drown! How long is this going to take?"

"Till we find the seals. Isn't it lovely? The wind, and all the sparkles?"

A Brownie leader, overhearing, smiled in agreement, but Gareth said stubbornly, "No. It's vile!"

After that he clamped his mouth tight shut, staring rigidly at the horizon.

"What's the matter?" demanded Binny.

"You KNOW what's the matter!"

"No one has been sick all summer," said Binny very firmly. "Have they, Liam?"

"No, and no one better be either," said Liam, whose horror of sickness was worse than all his horrors of stickiness, and chewing gum, and accidentally undercharging combined. "Everyone okay?" he called across to the Brownies, and looked relieved when they all stopped chattering to chorus, "Oh yes!"

"See, everyone's fine!" said Binny. All the same, after a sideways glance at Gareth, she could not help hoping that they would find the seals very quickly indeed.

This did not happen.

The seals were not in their sunny patch across the bay. Nor were they out on the island.

"How much farther?" asked Gareth.

"Hardly any distance," said Binny, now very worried. "Only just where we were this morning. That rocky point."

"Miles, then," said Gareth, white-faced.

"No. A few minutes. We're already more than halfway."

Gareth groaned.

"Hang on."

Gareth hung on. They reached the point, the engine slowed, seal heads bobbed and ducked inquisitively, and the enchanted Brownies snapped photos with disposable cameras. A Brownie leader wondered aloud what sort of seals they were, and Gareth roused enough to answer, "Atlantic Grays."

"Thank you! And those big diving gulls?"

"Gannets," said Gareth, and was well enough to add witheringly, "Not gulls at all!"

Liam, with the engine stopped, was allowing his boat to drift closer and closer in toward the rocks. A huge black bird suddenly took off and headed low over the water.

"Cormorant," said Gareth, looking better each moment. "Hang on! What's that?"

It was a blue nylon tangle of fish net, caught just above the waterline. Laced amongst it, clearly visible, seaweed, rubbish, fishing line with wicked hooks, and a pitiful bundle of white feathers.

Gareth pointed all these things out. The Brownie leaders also added loud, displeased remarks. The Brownies stopped looking enchanted and began to look distressed.

"Get in closer and unhook it," Gareth commanded Liam.

"Don't be daft," said Liam crossly. "I don't want that thing in the boat. Anyway, I couldn't. It's not safe any closer in."

"Let me get out, then!"

"Let you get out?" repeated Liam, staring at Gareth as if he was mad.

"It's not deep. I can see the bottom. I'll get the net, and if you don't want it in the boat, you can tow it behind."

Liam looked at Binny. His look said, *Tell me straight. Is he insane?*

"It wouldn't take ten minutes," said (the clearly insane) Gareth. "You make all this money exploiting the local wild-life . . ." (There was a murmur of agreement from the three Brownie leaders.) ". . . You should get out there and do something to help!"

"Look, mate," said Liam, in a gentle, lunatic-humoring voice. "It'll probably be gone on the next tide."

"What, do you think it's going to vanish or something?" demanded Gareth. "What if one of these seals gets tangled in it! Look at those hooks!"

"You're upsetting the Brownies!" hissed Binny furiously.

This was true. Some were round-eyed with dismay. Some were trying to shoo the seals out of range of Gareth's hor-rible net. Some were being restrained by their leaders from climbing into the water and fishing it out themselves. All their cheerful good manners had vanished. They were a potential explosion.

"Right, then, people!" called Liam, over all the rabble of noise that the Brownies were now creating. "I'll see about getting that bit of net sorted at the first opportunity (although as a matter of fact, it's probably been there for weeks doing no harm at all). But right now, we're all going home!"

"What?" shouted Gareth. "You're just turning away and leaving it?"

"Binny!" snapped Liam. "For anything's sake, *shut him up!*"

And then he shut him up himself by starting the engine.

They went home very fast indeed, and *The GoGettaGirl* did not like it. It made her bump and churn. It made her exhaust fumes turn blue and smell of diesel. It made the sea hit her in wet hard slaps.

Gareth didn't even notice the rainbows in the spray.

He went very quiet.

Started polishing his glasses.

Gave up.

Turned his face into the wind and took great gulps.

Clutched the side of the boat.

Fought the memory of warm squashed bananas, five slices of pizza, and the packet of ginger cream cookies.

Gurgled and heaved.

"Oh no, no, no!" begged Binny.

Everywhere.

Not into the water, into the wind.

Not once, but over and over.

A dreadful splattering rain began to shower over the boat and also over Gareth and the Brownies, Liam, and their leaders, the seats, and the life jackets. Not Binny, who at the first ominous noises had skipped prudently behind Liam, but everyone else.

Seasickness is catching. Very soon the Brownie leaders were grim and gray and the Brownies themselves terribly ill.

Liam was very restrained. He said nothing out loud that a Brownie should not hear. However, at the harbor, where beyond all hope they finally arrived, he gave an order.

"Get him off my boat," he said to Binny.

So Binny did.

Chapter Fourteen

Gareth climbed the harbor steps on all fours, like a beetle. When he reached the top he tottered across to the sheltering harbor wall, slumped down beside a pile of lobster pots, and groaned.

"Don't you be sick on those pots!" said Binny, scurrying around him like a cross little whirlwind. "You've caused enough trouble!"

Sounds of the trouble Gareth had caused came across from the seal trip boat. The Brownie leaders were driving hard bargains.

"Poor Liam," said Binny.

"Poor Liam!" repeated Gareth, at last strong enough to raise his aching head. "He ought to be arrested, driving a boat like that!"

"He's a very good boat driver!" said Binny indignantly. "Stop being so horrible, just because you were sick."

"Clear off and leave me alone, then. And don't moan

at me for being sick. It was all your rotten idea in the first place."

"I thought you'd like the lovely seals."

"Lovely seals!" repeated Gareth. "Fat lot you care about the lovely seals!"

"Of course I do, and so does Liam! He takes food to them every day!"

"They don't need food! They need that net getting rid of before one of them gets caught in it. He should do it, but I bet he never bothers. And neither will you."

"How could—?"

"Oh, leave it!" said Gareth, heaving himself to his feet. "I'm off."

"Didn't you like any of it?" asked Binny in a small voice.

"No, I didn't! You just dragged me out there to show off. Crew!" said Gareth scornfully. "Where's my bike?"

Binny jumped. She had forgotten the bike. Where was it? *You can't leave it there,* Liam had said. *Take it across to Kate.* All afternoon it had utterly vanished from her thoughts, but now, but now . . .

"Your bike!" exclaimed Binny, and turned and ran and when Gareth caught up with her she was halfway along the promenade, scurrying round and round a wooden seat.

"What's going on?" demanded Gareth.

"I left it here."

"*Here?*"

"Leaning." Binny rushed up the street, down again, circled the wooden seat once more, dropped on all fours and peered at the ground underneath, and then crumpled up onto the cobbled pavement, hugging her knees.

"You left it *here?*" demanded Gareth. "Where is it, then?"

"There was a dog . . . I didn't take it to Kate. There was a dog. Black and white. Not grown up. A big puppy."

Gareth was staring as if she was mad.

"With some people. And I suddenly thought, 'What if Aunty Violet . . .' So—"

"What if Aunty Violet, what?" interrupted Gareth.

"Nothing. It would take too long to explain. So I ran after them. The dog people."

"With my bike?"

"No. I left it by this bench. Just for a minute."

All the time Binny was speaking she was running. Up and down the promenade. Across to the harbor pier. Round all the wooden benches that stood primly bolted to the pavement, facing the sea.

"Stand still!" ordered Gareth, exhausted from keeping up with her. "Stand still and tell me what happened!"

"They were very nice. Their dog was called Bess. They

let me stroke her and they showed me how she shook paws. Then I remembered about the Brownies and I came back very quickly because Liam needed me to help him because I was . . ."

"Crew!" said Gareth bitterly. "You! Crew! What a joke! As if you could be trusted with anything!"

"I can."

"What, like my bike? It's been stolen, hasn't it? Like that Liam said would happen. Someone would have it the minute we left, he said, didn't he?"

Binny nodded. Forlorn.

"What am I going to tell my dad? I wasn't even supposed to be out with it!"

"I'll tell your dad," offered Binny.

"Oh, like he'll take it better coming from you!" exclaimed Gareth, turning furiously away and beginning to march up the hill toward home. "What're you going to say? You left it to run off after a dog? Do you know how insane that sounds?"

"I won't just say it like that. I'll explain."

"Oh yes! How?"

"I'll explain that I thought it was a dog I knew. My dog . . ."

"You don't have a dog!"

"My dog that I lost, I was going to say. My dog that Aunty Violet stole. Max."

Nothing Binny was saying was making anything better. Gareth's temper, with every word, with every step nearer home, was growing worse and worse. Now he suddenly spun round, stood quite still, and glared at Binny.

"You don't," he said, "have a dog called Max."

"I do! I did! But Aunty Violet stole him and gave him away!"

"I'm not interested."

"I've been looking for him ever since."

"I couldn't care less," said Gareth, spitting out the words as if they tasted bad.

"For years now."

"Will. You. Shut. Up!"

"I'm just explaining!" Binny scurried to keep up. "I'm sorry about your bike! I'm really sorry. But your dad can call the police and perhaps they will find it and I promise I will tell him it was all my fault."

They were nearly home. One more turn of the climbing cobbled street and their front doors would be before them. Gareth grabbed Binny's wrist, shoved her against a wall, and barred the way with his arm.

"Don't you go telling my dad anything!"

"What?"

"Don't you dare! Or anyone else!"

"But that's not fair!"

"It's nothing to do with fair. It's no one's business except mine. I'll say I left my bike and it got taken. You mind your own!"

"I shall have to tell my mum."

"Why? She going to buy another bike for me?"

Binny was silent, remembering her family's astonishment when she had reported the cost of Gareth's bike. *Eight hundred pounds?* James had asked. *That's a mort!*

There had been laughter then, but Binny did not feel like laughing now. She stared dumbly at Gareth.

"No," said Gareth, answering his own question. "She's not. So that's that."

He took his arm away and spoke almost wearily. "I'll tell my dad my bike got stolen. He'll go mad. She'll calm him down. He'll say she's an angel and whatever did we do without her. Vomit, vomit, vomit and everything will be lovely. So you keep out of it! All right?"

"Yes. All right. Thank you, Gareth."

"I don't want you to thank me," said Gareth, once more walking up the street.

"I'll do something to make it up to you, then. I'll make Liam get that net off the rocks."

"Yes, like Liam's going to be doing you favors anytime soon! I'll get it off myself. You keep out of it. You keep out of everything!"

"I'm not surprised you're mad," said Binny humbly.

Gareth growled.

"But I think you're being very kind about your bike."

"I am NOT being kind!" said Gareth, reached his own front door, marched inside, and slammed it very hard indeed.

Binny drooped a bit after that, down on the doorstep with her chin on her knees, and while she was there, the first rain of summer began to fall, first single drops, and then a steady, soaking downpour.

"Locked out?" inquired someone, hurrying past.

She shook her head.

"In you go, then."

"I'm fine."

Her hair became dark with water and more seaweedy than ever. At the end of the street a shape that might have been Aunty Violet appeared and dissolved.

"Binny, Binny, Bin!"

Her mother, home from work, exclaiming, warm despite the weather, hugging her.

"Drenched! You're drenched! What were you thinking of?"

"I wasn't thinking."

"You are so like your father!" said her mother, half in love, half in exasperation.

The door of the house was open. Warmth welled out, and a smell like heaven.

"I can't remember him. Not one little bit."

"You can. You will. I promise. Now, go and find something dry to wear and come down quickly. Rub your hair with a towel."

"Hello, don't kiss me," said James, appearing in Binny's bedroom doorway as she scrubbed at her hair. "Clem's been cooking and cooking. There's sausages, and chocolate gingerbread. I'm starving."

In the kitchen, watching Clem stuff roasted sausages into hot bread rolls, Binny found that she was starving too. Ravenous. Limp with hunger.

"There's two rolls each," said Clem, "but I only want one."

"Can I? Can I?" begged James, his hand hovering.

"Ask Binny if she wants half first."

"She had a whole pizza," said James, who had watched the picnic being packed very jealously that morning.

"Gareth ate it," said Binny, nevertheless pushing the last roll toward James. "All but one slice."

"And you took bananas."

"Gareth," said Binny.

"A whole packet of cookies."

"Gareth."

"Then did you go on the seal boat?"

"Mmmm. Are we having gingerbread for dessert?"

Clem put a plate piled high with warm squares in the middle of the table. James said, "Gareth told me boats made him sick."

"They do," said Binny. "Everywhere."

"Oh, Binny!" exclaimed her mother.

"There were fourteen Brownies," said Binny. "Please can I try some gingerbread, Clem?"

"Help yourself," replied Clem. "Fourteen Brownies on the boat?"

"Yes."

"They weren't all sick too?"

"I don't think all. They made an awful fuss, though. And some of them tried to get off the boat. It was terrible. Afterward the Brownie leaders made Liam give all their ticket money back. They argued for ages. They wouldn't go away until he did."

"What a pest you are, Binny!" said Clem suddenly.

"I don't see how it was Binny's fault," said their mother.

"She didn't know Gareth got seasick, I don't suppose, and anyway, she didn't make him go on the boat . . ."

"Didn't she?" asked Clem, marching out of the room.

"Did you, Bin?" asked her mother, and then, at the sight of Binny's guilty bowed head and crimson ear tips, "Oh! Then you *are* a pest! After Liam's been so kind! And poor Gareth!"

"I never thought he'd really be sick," said Binny. "I thought he was making it up."

"Well, now you know you were wrong, and I hope you've apologized!"

"That's all I've been doing for hours and hours and hours."

"Good. Now, since Clem cooked and I've been at work all day . . ."

"I'll clear up the kitchen," said Binny.

"Thank you. And James will help." She left, and James, who was usually the one labeled pest, looked at Binny and smirked.

"I've been good all day," he remarked. "Good in the garden. Good being very kind to seagulls . . ." James paused to give himself another piece of gingerbread. "Good helping Clem."

"Marvelous old you," said Binny.

"I think Gareth got in trouble for being sick. I heard his dad shouting."

"When?"

"Before you came in with Mum. In the garden. Then she came out and calmed him down."

"Yes. Gareth said she would."

Clem made her gingerbread with melted butter and golden syrup, and then, at the last minute before baking, frozen chocolate chips that melted into dark chocolate swirls. It was impossible to eat it and not feel better. Binny reached for a second piece and James said happily, "You'll never guess what I've got in the bathroom."

"What?"

"Instead of chickens. I thought I'd try them."

"What?"

"I got 'em in by opening the window wide as wide and putting bread on the windowsill."

"James?"

"First they wouldn't land properly and just grabbed bits. But then one came right in and another one followed it. And I closed the window really quick and I got them both. I haven't told Mum and Clem yet. It's a surprise. I'm waiting till they lay eggs. I've made nests in the bath . . ."

James paused, listening.

Footsteps on the stairs. A great shriek from Clem. A sound like mad burglars trying to tear off the roof.

"JAMES! JAMES! JAMES!"

"I thought you said you'd been good all day," said Binny.

Two gulls like wild screeching angels.

"They *weren't* that big before!" wailed James, fleeing to his bedroom.

Afterward, after the huge clean-up, Binny and Clem put the buckets and mops away and loaded the washing machine with everyone's towels, while their mother shoved James into bed.

"And stay there!" she ordered.

"Yes," said James humbly. "Mummy?"

Rarely, only on the brink of sleep, did James say "Mummy" anymore.

"Mmm?"

"Seagulls didn't work."

"They didn't really, James."

"Chickens, then."

"One day."

"Yes," said James, and tumbled over the brink and into sleep.

"Don't kiss me," his mother heard him murmur from that far place, and wondered who he'd met.

★ ★ ★

"Bedtime, you two," she told Clem and Binny, when she finally came downstairs. "Off you go! Tomorrow is a bright new day."

Her words made a picture in Binny's mind as she lay in bed that night. A wide blue morning sky. A shimmering sea. Sunlight. A tide-smoothed, empty beach.

Binny's imagination sailed happily into this pleasant world and added extras.

A repentant bicycle thief.

An apologetic Gareth. *(It was all my fault for guzzling all that pizza!)*

A sudden fortune for Liam and a new boat, sparkling clean and with a new name, *SWEET BELINDA* in curly white letters on the fresh paint. *"You don't mind, do you, Binny? I couldn't resist."*

"It's lovely, Liam. Of course I don't mind."

Bury your face in Max's fur to hide your blushes.

Chapter Fifteen

They woke to a morning as gray as November.

James was astonished. Until now, he had never experienced any seaside weather but sunshine. Rain and the seaside seemed as unlikely an event as a midnight rainbow or an indoor wind. He scrambled into his wetsuit and rushed outside to investigate and found that it had turned his world upside down. His sheep farm was flooded and the livestock afloat. All his high tide marks had vanished from the fence, and his lettuce had changed form entirely and burst into small yellow flowers.

"Wow!" said James, impressed.

The holidaymakers were not impressed at all. Rain outraged them, swept them off the beaches, swirled them into a grumbling tideline, and washed them into the little town. They arrived looking mutinous and belligerent, like people who are sure they are about to be cheated. They took the rain personally, saying things like, *Just our luck!*

There was nothing anybody could say to please them. They were infuriated to hear, *It hasn't rained properly since May.* Their usual reply to that was, *And it had to pick this one week!*

Kate's café filled to bursting with damp people. Clem and Binny were welcome every day to help out. Binny soon found herself following Kate's example of dispensing imaginary, very positive weather forecasts.

"After this bit of . . . of fog and stuff . . . it's going to get hotter 'n' hotter," she would assure customers earnestly, ignoring the streaming windows, drenched on the outside with torrential rain, and on the inside with equally torrential condensation. "It's the best weather to see seals," she told people (following instructions from Liam). "We can . . . you can get closer."

"Much closer?" they asked.

"Oh yes," said Binny, who would have said anything for Liam. Wonderfully, Liam had forgiven her, and was already telling the story of Gareth and the Brownies as a good joke against himself. "Oh yes, much closer! Right up to them, almost."

"Is it a covered boat?"

"Covered in what? Oh! With a roof, you mean? Not actually . . . No, not an awning either. You could take umbrellas. Or raincoats. Or hats."

For all her trying, Binny did not manage to convince many people of the charms of seal trips in open boats and pouring rain. *The GoGettaGirl* hardly left the shelter of the harbor, and her owner spent his time as a temporary cook and coffee machine operator, much to his sister's surprise.

"He usually spends wet days in the pub," she said, "making half a pint last all afternoon . . . Still . . . The kittens are ready to go, Binny, did I tell you? The two spotty ones went yesterday and I could have given yours away over and over. She's by far the prettiest."

"I know. Don't give her away!"

"Of course I won't, but she ought to go soon. The trouble is there should be someone at home with her the first few days and your Mum's at work, and Clem's here."

"There's me."

"Wouldn't you get lonely? Would that boy . . . Gareth? . . . come round and keep you company?"

Binny shook her head. Gareth no longer climbed the garden fence or hung out of his bedroom window, waiting to do battle. To Binny he had become a brooding fury, an angry invisible presence on the other side of her bedroom wall. Once, out with James to choose turnovers for supper, she had met him in the street. Then his darkness had become obliterating. He had shown no signs of having seen them, but she had felt the disturbance of his passing like electricity in the air.

James, wet and cheerful, had not seemed aware of this at all, and he had noticed something that Binny had not spotted.

"Wait!" James had called, and dashed back up the street and into the shadows that hung around Gareth.

Then it had seemed to Binny that for a minute or two the air had brightened. The rain had glimmered on James's round cherub face as he jiggled in front of his friend, tropical bright in his wetsuit. Watching, Binny had seen James fling wide his arms as if telling marvels. She saw Gareth give his old half-rueful grin. Then James had come racing back to her, and when she glanced back that way again, the darkness was as dense as ever.

Although still invisible to James.

"He's hurt his arm again," he told Binny. "The one he broke. He fell on his shoulder, getting out of his window. The rain made the windowsill slippery. It's not broken, though. But it hurts and he's got to wear that thing. That sling thing."

"Oh. Poor Gareth."

"He's all right, though. And he said not to get chicken

and mushroom because it's got mushrooms in it, but I wasn't going to anyway."

"What? What are you talking about?"

"Turnovers!" James told her happily, and he had recited the menu as he hopped the puddles. "Lambanmint, chickenanmushroom, chickentikka, cheeseanvegetable, mediterraneanvegan, goldenoriginal, goldenoriginal-whopper, that's mine!"

"Is that really all you talked about?"

"And his arm."

"Nothing about me?"

"'Course not. You're dumped, aren't you?"

"DUMPED! Me! By Gareth! We're not even friends!"

"You can dump your enemies too," said James.

The white kitten came home and all the white kitten names they had thought of that summer were trumped by James who said, "Cinderella!"

"Cinderella?" asked everyone, and they looked at the kitten.

The kitten looked expectantly back at them.

"Like in the story," said James.

"It's perfect," said Clem.

"It's just right," agreed Binny. "Cinderella. Cinderella,

Cinderella!" she called, and swung a white seagull feather on a string so that the kitten scampered and rolled in somersaults and purred with pleasure.

"How did you come to think of it, James?" they asked admiringly.

"'Cos of her two ugly sisters," said James.

Binny and Cinderella stayed at home through the rainy days, while James went to work with his mother, and Clem learned to balance soup bowls and make toasted sandwiches. Binny was all right on the first day, when the sounds from next door, slamming doors and shouted rudeness, cheered the quietness of the hours. However, the next day, when Gareth and his family seemed to have all gone out in a huff, it was different. Cinderella fell asleep, the rain darkened the windows, and Binny began the dangerous activity of thinking too much.

Beginning with the ominous, *Here I am, all alone in Aunty Violet's house.*

Tight and white the kitten slept, locked in another, safer world. Outside, a gusty wind found the chimney pot and called down echoes. Binny's reckless thinking reached the always disastrous point of, *Nobody would hear me if I screamed.*

The letterbox rattled, Binny jumped, and Aunty Violet

age sixteen, recently banished to a shadowy corner of the bookshelf, suddenly became a presence in the room.

So, she demanded, fixing Binny firmly with her gaze, *how does it feel when your wishes come true?*

Binny scooped up the kitten and held it like a shield, but Aunty Violet's eyes were still upon her.

Dead. This hair that looked like your hair. These eyes that looked like your eyes. These hands.

"You'd have died anyway," answered Binny, not out loud but thought to thought, the way she always spoke to Aunty Violet. "You were old."

Oh? said Aunty Violet, not looking old at all.

All at once Binny had had enough. She backed out of the room, grabbed her jacket from the hook by the door, zipped the kitten inside, and fled the shadowy house. Down the rainy streets she ran, along the salt-sprayed seafront, and into the crowded coffee warmth of the café.

"Kate! Kate!" she wailed, weaving between tables and strollers and damp-smelling holidaymakers.

"Kate, Liam, Clem!"

Liam and Clem appeared simultaneously from the back of the room. Kate came reversing through the doors carrying an incredible amount of china.

"What ever is the matter?" asked Clem.

"Aunty Violet!"

"Who the heck is Aunty Violet?" demanded Liam. "That's not what you called the cat, is it, Clemency?"

Clem batted him with a menu for calling her Clemency and told him, "Aunty Violet is Binny's ancient enemy! Binny, did you lock the house?"

"Oh," said Binny.

"I knew! We'll be burgled!"

"I just ran out," said Binny, and ran back and found the house not only unburgled, but occupied by her mother and James and a lettuce crate, begged from a market stall.

"Hello, don't kiss me, look what I've got!" said James. "It's for making into a henhouse."

"Binny, the door was wide open!" said her mother, hugging her. "You mustn't leave it like that! Have you been all right?"

"Yes," said Binny, glancing warily across at Aunty Violet as she unzipped the kitten. "I'm sorry about the door. I just ran down to Kate's for a minute. Is that box really big enough for chickens?"

"It's big enough for imaginary ones," said her mother. "Isn't it, James?"

James, already busy on the floor with cardboard and tape, smiled inscrutably up at her. He patched up the holes in the lettuce box and added a door with tape hinges. Later, in his bedroom, he labeled each of the four inside corners with a stern instruction: *EAT. DRINK. POO. EGGS.*

"But how will the chickens understand?" objected Binny. "Chickens can't read."

"I'll read the notices and then it'll understand," said James.

"You've done really well," said Binny, getting down on her knees to admire it properly. "The door's extra good, the way you've made it open and shut."

"I wish it would stop raining, though," said James.

"Well, can't you keep it here in your bedroom, until it stops raining?"

"In here?" asked James, looking astonished.

"Why not? It doesn't take up that much space."

"No," agreed James. "It wouldn't take up that much space."

"Rain would ruin it."

James nodded.

"And I don't suppose invisible chickens like getting wet."

"Visible ones don't," said James.

Thoughtfully.

They both became silent, gazing at the chicken house. And presently, they both smiled. Binny smiled because she had just had the good idea of secretly smuggling a real egg into the chicken house. She imagined how she would place it, tidily in the correct corner. An egg under *EGGS*. A visible surprise from the invisible occupants.

James smiled because he was thinking of his mort.

The Rock Pools V

"Climb!" said Gareth.

They climbed, not just out of reach of the waves, but to the highest point of the miniature island that the headland had become. There the rocks were still warm and dry, and the sea was a serene summer blue, and even the swirling patch of whiteness between themselves and the shore looked sparklingly unthreatening.

"Wow, we were stupid!" groaned Gareth.

"Yes," agreed Binny. "Do you want to try again?"

"What did you say?"

"Do you want to try again?"

"No."

"What, then?"

Gareth did not reply.

"Anyway, it's warm," said Binny. The warmth was lovely after the icy incoming tide. She could see a seal. They had rescued the net. It was just a matter of waiting until the sea went down again. Making the best of things.

"Hell. Rubbish. No," said Gareth, hunched with his back to her, not making the best of anything.

"What's the matter?"

"Phone. Soaked."

"Won't it switch on?"

"It's switched on, but nothing's happening."

"Can I look?" asked Binny, reaching out a hand, and Gareth jerked away so quickly that the sodden bundle of sock bandage came loose.

"Why won't you ever share your phone?"

"Look what happened when I shared my bike! Okay, okay, don't look like that! Do you think my arm looks swollen?"

"No," said Binny, and added, because of the unnecessary remark about the bike, "it's just as skinny as the other one!"

"It's bleeding again."

"Not much," said Binny. "Nothing like before. Shall I tie the bandage back on?"

"It's not a bandage, it's a mucky sock. And no, thanks, look at it! I've probably got blood poisoning already. It feels like I have."

"How do you know what blood poisoning feels like?"

"I've had it before. I've had blood poisoning, bronchitis, broken arm, broken leg, concussion, chicken pox, an ear thing that lasted ages, three teeth out, stitches in my neck . . ."

"Your neck?"

"I walked through a window. And now drowning!"

"You're not drowning!"

"Not yet."

"The sea will go down soon."

"It hasn't finished coming up yet."

"Hasn't it?" asked Binny. "Gareth! Do you think these rocks go under the sea?"

"Do you mean, do I think the sea goes over these rocks?"

"Yes," said Binny in such a frightened voice that Gareth was sorry he'd mentioned drowning.

"Oh well, if it does, we'll just swim," he said, as casually as he could. "Or float," he added, in response to Binny's squeak of dismay. "That's all we'd have to do, really, and the tide would wash us in."

"Let's not think about it until we have to," said Binny. "Talk about something else! Did you really walk through a window?"

"Yes, and I was knocked over by a van in the street! That's when they found out I needed glasses. They might have guessed. I'd already walked through the window by then."

"Who might have guessed?"

"Mum and Dad. Too busy fighting. They're split now."

"Poor you."

"It was ages ago."

"It must have been awful."

"That last summer we were here, I used to hide. Over the fence in your garden."

Just as Gareth spoke, Binny saw something flash in his hand. His phone, flickering back to life. They both jumped and Gareth's fingers closed tight.

"Is it working?" asked Binny as he bent over it.

"Yes. No. No, it's not. Screen's frozen."

"There's a picture."

"It's nothing."

"You've gone red."

"I haven't," said Gareth, but he had.

Chapter Sixteen

Letters began to arrive for Binny. She opened them in private.

We are very sorry to inform you . . . they began, and continued equally depressingly. *No record . . . No knowledge . . .* Words like that. They ended kindly: *We do hope . . . We wish you every success . . .* Binny screwed them up and hurled them at Aunty Violet's photograph (recently repositioned by Binny herself on a dingy shelf at the top of the stairs where a very large spider had been spotted).

Aunty Violet saved her revenge until the middle of the night, when she hurled herself down the stairs in a series of clatters that half scared Binny to death. Clem and James thought this was very funny and clever of Aunty Violet, but Binny did not.

"I can't bear living with her any longer!" she said, and made a private expedition to the trash can. A few minutes later she shrieked with horror when she discovered that

Aunty Violet, looking supernaturally complacent, had reappeared on the kitchen table.

"Of course I got her out," said Clem, coming into the kitchen to find her sister walking backward and pointing. "You can't put Aunty Violet in the trash!"

Binny put her in a bag instead, and took her down to Kate's, and Kate was wonderful.

"Of course we should love to have her!" she exclaimed, when she had untangled Binny's tale of spiders, letters, trash cans, and despair. "I'm sorry you didn't have good news, but don't give up just yet. I've found two vets near where your granny lived. I've got their addresses here."

Binny thanked her for the addresses, cleared some tables, learned how to make an Ice-Cold Strawberry Surfer, ate it, and cheered up. In a brief gap between customers she and Kate found Aunty Violet a very honorable place in the café picture gallery, left of Elvis Presley and directly above Prince Charles.

"Next to Elvis!" she told Aunty Violet encouragingly, polishing her with a paper napkin and avoiding her eyes. "That's quite posh. He was a very famous . . . very famous . . . Liam! What was Elvis Presley famous for?"

"Crikey, Binny," said Liam, heading for the door. "Don't you know anything?"

"No. Where are you going?"

"Harbor. Taking some lunatics fishing in the rain."

"Oh. Without me?"

"Definitely," said Liam, with a briskness utterly unlike the Liam of her dreams.

"Liam, you know that net?"

"Not again!"

"Is it still there?"

"How would I know?"

"What about Elvis?"

"I don't know where he is either," said Liam, and left so swiftly it looked like an escape.

It was now Binny's sixth full day without her enemy, and she was surprised how much she missed him. Now, when she looked out in the mornings, she did it alone. The window next to her own remained glassily closed, and all day long it stayed that way. Not that Gareth had vanished. Nor did he seem to be missing Binny. Far from it. He was very busy, Binny could tell, making life intolerable for everyone else.

It was like living next door to an imprisoned thunderstorm.

Raging explosions and long, fuming silences. Doors slammed so hard you could hear the wood split. In the evenings, when the rain eased off, a solitary figure pacing in the garden.

"Poor thing!" said Clem.

"Her?" asked Binny indignantly. Gareth might be the enemy. He might have dumped her. But still, in the end, she was on his side.

"She's the worst thing that ever happened to him," she told Clem solemnly.

"But why?"

"She does his head in. She hates everything he likes."

"Does Gareth actually like anything, then?" asked Clem. "I don't think I've ever heard him do anything but complain."

"He likes lots of things!" said Binny defensively. "He likes animals; you know he does!"

"She hates them!" said James, who was listening. "Gareth told me. Cats, dogs, rabbits, all the animals, she hates! We'd better be careful of Cinders."

They looked at Cinders, asleep on the sofa, curled into a perfect circle, like a snow-white rose.

"Nothing will happen to Cinders," said Clem. "She's no trouble to anyone. Not like . . ."

Clem paused.

"Max," said Binny. "I know what you were going to say!

Max was a million times more exciting, though. Cinders is too good."

Cinders stirred in her sleep. Perhaps she heard. Perhaps she agreed. She wasn't very good the next morning.

She vanished.

By the end of the week the steady rain had stopped. Instead they had showers, sudden and sparkling, with proper seaside hotness in between. This weather caused the chopped-back jungle that was Aunty Violet's garden to explode into life. One morning Cinderella slipped through the back door, paused, stared in astonishment at this strange new greenness, and melted into it as quickly as a handful of snow in a tropical landscape.

"Cinders, Cinders, Cinderella!" called Binny, tangled by briars, ambushed by spiders, crawling on all fours amongst the soaking, snail-infested grasses.

Sometimes there was a rustle, sometimes a flash of white, but no actual Cinders.

"Cinders!" begged Binny, for about the millionth time, and a voice from above said, "Excuse me," and it was her.

"Excuse me," said the voice, "but have you lost a kitten? If so, I think we may have her in the house."

She was very thin, and dressed in the sort of long, floating skirt that Binny's own mother never had the time to wear. Her voice was raspy, as if she'd been coughing.

"A white kitten," she said. "In the sitting room. You're Gareth's friend, aren't you? Would you like to come over and collect her?" Binny, suddenly dumb, nodded, climbed the apple tree, dropped down on the other side of the fence, and found herself in a different world.

"I'm afraid Gareth's out with his father at the moment," the woman said, leading Binny to doors that opened into a room like an illustration from an expensive magazine. "I'm sorry, but I wish you would take her away as soon as you can. I have quite a problem with cats, as well as dogs."

She motioned Binny in, but stepped no farther than the doorway herself. "She was by the piano," she told Binny, and at that moment Binny spotted Cinders. Her small face was gazing up with an expression of absolute glee, and she mewed when Binny stepped toward her.

"Don't worry about your shoes!"

My shoes! Binny looked down and saw a line of muddy footprints on a pale gray carpet. Hurriedly she pulled them off and there were her bare feet, almost as bad. Perhaps, thought Binny in a chain of panic-stricken thoughts, I should go home, wash them . . . No that's silly! Get Cinders first, say sorry, come back, and help clear up . . .

"Oh dear!" said the voice at the door.

"Cinders!"

Fast as lightning, Cinders had swapped her corner by the piano for the open fireplace. There she crouched, hardly visible behind an arrangement of blue sea holly. The moment Binny reached out her hand, she sprang lightly up the chimney, and vanished.

Soot fell, blackening the sea holly. Then Cinders came tumbling down again, eluded Binny very neatly, and by way of a bookcase and the back of the sofa, scuttled to the top of the curtain rail.

The horrible crack that came as Binny tried to retrieve Cinderella from the curtains was the rail coming from the wall. It did far more damage than anything that fell afterward: a few silvery shells arranged in a glass, some papers, and a set of speakers.

"Perhaps if you were to stop chasing her."

Binny, who had almost forgotten that she and Cinders were not alone, paused in surprise. Cinderella paused too. Her round kitten eyes looked about the room in astonishment, as if to ask, *Whatever happened here?* She sat down, noticed her paws, washed one, stretched, strolled happily across the room, and rubbed her small dirty head against Binny's ankles.

Purring.

"Actually a darling little thing," Binny heard, as she scooped up Cinders at last. "Don't worry about the room. It wasn't your fault. I wish I could have helped you but I'm so terribly ..."—she puffed on a blue asthma inhaler— "...allergic."

"Oh!" said Binny, the first word she had spoken during the whole appalling episode, but before she could say more the pale woman was speaking again. "I shall have to . . ." she began, coughed, waved briefly, and vanished around a corner of the house.

"Allergic," said Binny to Clem. "And do you know what she called Cinders? A darling little thing! That's weird, isn't it?"

"I think it's very nice of her, considering!" said Clem.

James spent the same day with the chickens at the old people's home, feeding them to bursting point with chicken food, woodlice, and snails. He fed them so much that by the end of the afternoon they could hardly be bothered to cluck.

Then James went home with his mother.

She was worrying. There was a sudden staff crisis at the home and they had asked if she could work that night.

"How would you feel if I went back after supper?" she asked Binny and Clem when she arrived home. "Do you think you could manage?"

"Work all day and then all night?" exclaimed Binny. "That's awful!"

"It's not so much working as just being there if they need me. I could take tomorrow off to catch up. But it would mean leaving Clem in charge here. Could you manage, Clem? Were you planning on doing something this evening?"

"Only going down to Kate's. That doesn't matter. I don't mind staying in. I might start painting my bedroom. I've got the paint."

"If you're painting this evening, you should sleep downstairs tonight," said her mother. "Away from the smell while it's drying. And James and Binny had better keep their doors shut too. You'll all have headaches otherwise. I'll ring up and say I can help, then. As long as James behaves. Where is he? He's gone."

"I'm here!" James appeared, looking preoccupied. When they explained the plans for later, he did not seem a bit upset about the thought of being without his mother all night.

"Can you be good?" asked his mother, hugging him.

He nodded, leaning against her, sucking his fingers.

"Me and Clem will babysit you," said Binny. "Or perhaps just me, if Clem's painting!"

"I don't need babysitting!" protested James. "Mum, tell her I don't need babysitting!"

"Someone's got to put you to bed," said his mother.

"I can put myself to bed!" said James. "I'm six!"

"Yes, but will you?" asked his mother.

"'Course he won't," said Binny.

"'Course I will!" said James, and when the time came, he did, his bedroom door firmly closed and all offers of help and stories declined.

"Night night, don't kiss me," he remarked, appearing briefly in Clem's room, where his sisters were busy.

"Night, night, we weren't going to," replied Binny.

"We'll come and tuck you up in a while," promised Clem.

"No, don't," said James ungratefully.

Clem raised her eyebrows.

"I'm listening to *Harry Potter*," explained James, "so I'm busy. And I'm keeping my door shut 'cos this paint smells terrible."

"It's not that bad."

"It is. And it's a funny color too. What's it meant to be?"

"Smoke gray."

"It's purple."

"It's not!"

"Bluey-purple! Moldy."

"Moldy!"

"Do you want me to tell you where the drips are?"

"No."

"Okay."

"Where, then? Where are the drips? I thought I'd been so careful!"

James squinted, scrutinizing the room, and then pointed to a very small drip on Binny.

"That? That!"

He nodded.

"Oh, go to bed!" exclaimed Clem crossly. "Have you cleaned your teeth?"

"Yes," said James, opening his mouth wide and showing them all.

"Washed?"

"'Course."

"What?" asked Binny skeptically. "You took that wetsuit off, washed, and then put it on again?"

"Night, night," said James diplomatically, and slid away. They heard his door close, and then the heavy scrape of his chest of drawers being pulled across it as a barrier, and then *Harry Potter,* very loud.

"He was so sweet when he was little," said Binny. "Do you remember?"

"Hmm."

Time passed.

Binny, who had only been allowed to paint in the most obscure corners of the room, put down her brush.

"I'm done," she announced tiredly, and curled up on Clem's bed to watch her sister finish the final wall.

"Does it look moldy?" asked Clem suddenly.

Binny's eyes jerked open. "What? Oh, moldy! No. Well. No."

"It won't when it dries."

"Oh, good," said Binny and she let her eyes close once more and when she opened them again, it was dark outside and she was in her own bed.

"I put you there," said Clem from the doorway. "You can get washed in the morning. Like James."

Binny sighed with relief.

"Night, then, Bin."

"Ni . . ." began Binny, and did not finish.

Blackness. Smothering. Heavy and dark. The bedclothes twisted into shrouds. Noise all around. Whisper. Shuffle. A hard, repeated rap. *Rap.*

Clawing, like nails against plaster or wood.

★ ★ ★

Loudest of all, Binny's drumbeat heartbeat pounding so hard her ears sang with the pressure. Her body felt flattened as if by a great weight.

Buried.

Dead.

Another Aunty Violet nightmare.

Wake up.

Binny forced open her eyes, pushed down the quilt, and rolled her head on the pillow to shake the sleep away.

The sounds from her nightmare remained.

It can't be real, it can't be real, it can't be real.

The clawing was frantic.

Mum! begged Binny silently.

Often in the past her mother had seemed to hear these silent nightmares. She would come and say "Binny" and her hands would be cool as water. *Mum,* begged Binny again, and remembered.

Well, then, Clem.

Clem was not like her mother, Clem could be summoned by nothing more than terrible need. Clem would have to be sought out, and she was not near either. She was sleeping downstairs.

A soft, dragging, rasping sound, and again, the *rap, rap.*

Fearfully, clutching her quilt around her, Binny slid out of bed, reached her bedroom door, and crept down the stairs to find Clem.

Never in her life had she been more shocked than she was the next moment.

There, in the predawn gray light of the living room.

Asleep on the sofa.

Cinderella.

Clem.

Liam.

LIAM!

Shatteringly,

Liam.

Binny fled. Through the kitchen. Struggling with the outside door. Still clutching her quilt, tumbling and stumbling into the tangled garden and through dew and seeding grasses and the catching thorns of bramble bushes until she reached the apple tree.

In the pearl gray light the spread of the branches looked immense and the landscape of their leaves closed protectively around Binny as she climbed. She reached her surfboard platform, tugged her quilt up behind her, and sighed with relief. There were no nightmares here.

After a while she lay down, wrapped in her quilt, wedged

tight against the friendly roughness of the tree trunk, and she thought, Here I am.

And slept.

Once she woke with a jerk and a thumping heart. *Aunty Violet,* she thought, *and Liam, Clem.*

She remembered things: You can bring Clem for free if you like. The evening she rushed into the café, and they appeared simultaneously. *Clemency,* and, *What a pest you are, Binny!* Lots of things.

But they seemed very far away, and soon she settled again.

The hens in the chicken house at the old people's home could not settle. A strange new object had appeared amongst them. They turned their heads to regard it.

Dangerous, or not?

Edible, or not?

It unsettled them. They stepped warily around it, and their voices were anxious. They had had a disturbing day.

First, the loss.

The chickens could not count, but they knew, as well as they knew their own feathers, that there had been, and still was, a loss.

And now. This object. This nameless thing. This mystery.

It should not have been a mystery. James had certainly tried to explain.

"My mort."

The puzzle of how to turn his mort into chickens had worried James for some time. Clem, when she was turning her possessions into flute lessons, had worked her alchemy in stages. Possessions to money. Money to lessons.

It was the money stage that bothered James, for although it was his own mort, gathered by his own hard work from the disregarded belongings of his friends, he feared there might be questions when it came to the transformation.

Hard questions.

James thought and thought and the answer came to him like a sudden light turning on in his head.

Skip the money.

Take the mort to the chickens.

Hide it in the henhouse.

Choose a chicken.

Hide it in my bag with my sheep and things.

Carry it home and put it in my bedroom like Binny said I could.

Wait until any chicken-losing, mort-discovering fuss has died away.

Move the chicken to the garden.

"Goodness!" Clem and Binny and his mum would then say. "There's a lovely chicken living in the garden!"

"Is there?" James would ask. "Oh yes. Oh, good."

The first part of this plan had worked out very well indeed. Just before it was time to set off for home with his mother, James took his mort from his sheep bag, stowed it in a nest box, disguised it with straw, chose for himself the largest, doziest chicken, and lifted her out. She fit nicely into his sheep bag, where she was quiet and good, but remarkably heavy.

Ordinarily his mother would have seen that the sheep bag had swollen to twice its usual size. Probably she would have noticed the triumphant expression on James's face as well, and the way he hugged his heavy burden to his jubilant, fast-beating heart. But this day, wondering whether she could safely leave the family for the night, she did not.

James got the chicken home, past his sisters ("Hello, don't kiss me!"), and up the stairs. His plan reached the put-it-in-your-bedroom stage and then it began to hit problems.

Not for a moment would the chicken consent to live in the lettuce-crate chicken house. She ignored James's carefully written instructions *(EAT. DRINK. POO. EGGS.)* and marched straight out the door. That was when the problems began.

The poo problem.

The rummaging-through-everything-like-a-burglar problem.

The trying-to-fly problem.

And later, when bedtime came, the toe-attacking problem, the wanting-to-sit-on-the-highest-thing-possible (which happened to be the headboard of James's cabin bed) problem, and the staying-up-all-night problem.

It was a wonder that the other people in the house did not hear these problems, but they did not. Binny was asleep, bound in her nightmares. Clem was downstairs, and so was Liam, and they both had other things on their minds.

James was quite alone with his difficulties, and long before midnight he had begun to detest chickens. Especially the fat smelly enormous one that had taken over his room.

Her name, James remembered, was Gertie.

Gertie did not detest James. Quite the opposite; she insisted on staying very close to him indeed, either perched on the headboard of his bed, with her feathery bottom looming far too close to his face, or at the foot, from which point she insisted on trying to eat his toes, diving like a falcon every time they twitched. Socks did not deter her in the slightest, so James was forced to add shoes. Shoes puzzled poor Gertie so much that she walked about all over James, trying to work them out.

At about half past twelve at night James, desperate, removed the trapdoor to the attic, picked up Gertie, pushed her into the lettuce-crate chicken house, and stowed her in the attic. After that he fell asleep, and he did not wake until dawn, and the terrible sound of somebody laying an egg somewhere over his head.

But where?

By standing on tiptoe on his cabin bed, James could just see into the attic.

By adding his bedside chair, he could rest his elbows on the edge of the dark hole and look more carefully.

With a little heaving and kicking from this position he could climb right inside.

There was no proper floor, just ceiling joists and plaster, with a few planks here and there, making narrow paths to things like water tanks and wiring. The only light was a thin grayness that crept in from the eaves to illuminate three hundred years' worth of cobwebs, the skeleton of an ancient rat, the remains of the chicken house, and Gertie,

her orange feathers faintly glowing in the shadows like the last embers of a bonfire.

Gertie had had a lovely exciting night hunting spiders and tossing about rat bones. She had dismantled the chicken house, terrified Binny out of her bed, and laid an egg where no egg had ever been laid before, and now she was in a wild and silly mood. She would not be caught.

"You're the worst chicken in the world," said James, and he whimpered a little as he crawled after her because the attic joists hurt his knees so much, and the shadows in the corners were so dark.

Gertie seemed pleased to be the worst chicken. She behaved in a worst-chicken way, hopping and prinking, creating cobweb avalanches to fall on James's neck, and occasionally jabbing holes in the plaster with her beak. James struggled after her, brandishing the remains of the chicken house. The attic seemed enormous, much bigger than the house beneath, and it was very hot there too. James had almost reached the point when the only reasonable thing left to do seemed to be to lie on his stomach and howl, when a miracle happened. A square of light, Gertie startled into stillness, and a familiar voice demanding, "What the flipping heck..."

"Gareth!" cried James.

"That's a chicken!"

"Yes. Catch it! It's a terrible chicken, it won't let me near!"

"Catch it?"

"Just grab."

Gareth grabbed and was successful, and clambered down from the chest of drawers on which he was balanced.

"Put her in a bag!" ordered James.

"What bag?"

"Any bag!"

Gareth looked wildly round his bagless room, seized his pillow, tugged off the pillowcase, and lowered Gertie inside.

"Perfect," said James approvingly, and a minute later he was in the room too, hugging his knees on the end of Gareth's bed, and relating in a husky whisper all the horrible problems of chicken keeping, at night, indoors, in secret.

"But whose chicken is she?" asked Gareth when James finally paused for breath.

"Mine, but I don't want her. I'm giving her back."

"Back where?" asked Gareth.

"To the old ladies."

"You stole this chicken from the old people's home?"

"Not stole. Swapped."

"Swapped for what?" demanded Gareth.

"For my mort."

"Your *what*?"

A little uncomfortably, James explained the nature and acquisition of a mort.

"Crikey," said Gareth.

"Crikey what?"

"Does your mum know about this stuff?"

"'Course she doesn't! She'd never have . . ." James stopped.

"Carry on," said Gareth ominously.

". . . let me," said James, in a very small voice indeed.

There was a long silence. Gertie dozed inside her pillow-case. James sucked his fingers. Gareth looked smug, the way people who are in perpetual trouble do look smug when somebody else is caught.

James sighed.

"You should take her back," said Gareth severely. "Now. Before anyone knows she's gone."

James nodded.

"And all that stuff, you'll have to give it back to whoever it came from."

"My mort," said James, and bowed his head so that his small brown neck showed bare and vulnerable, a sight that invariably caused his mother and sisters to cave in and agree to his most unreasonable demands, but which had hardly any effect on Gareth at all.

"Come on. Be really quiet and I'll let you out," he said.

"Then what?" asked James, not raising his head.

"Then I'm going back to bed."

The limp eloquence of James's neck spread to his shoulders and he rubbed his eyes with his wrists.

"Hurry up," said Gareth, yawning as he stood over him.

James did not move.

"Oh, *what's* the matter?" growled Gareth.

"That chicken's so heavy. And my mort. All for nothing. Even the ruby."

"I bet there wasn't really a ruby," said Gareth scornfully. "Do you even actually know what a ruby is?"

"Red," said James, and a tear fell, a real tear, achieved by an enormous effort of will. It glimmered in the early light on Gareth's posh wooden floor.

It worked.

"All right, I'll come with you," said Gareth, and was immediately dazzled by a James transformation of such radiance that he was out of the house and halfway down the street before he stopped blinking.

James scurried after him, suddenly rather anxious.

"Does it hurt your bad arm much, carrying Gertie? Will you get in trouble? Why did nobody notice us, creeping out of your house?"

"What? Oh, they sleep miles away. On the other side of the stairs. They can't hear me and I can't hear them. Thank goodness."

"I could hear them," said James. "When we were going downstairs, I could."

"What did you hear?"

"Snoring."

Gareth grinned.

"And, stop walking a minute, Gareth! Listen! And crying. Her."

"Oh well, she does that a lot," said Gareth easily, peering into the pillowcase to see how Gertie was doing. "Doesn't mean a thing."

James stared at him, wide-eyed. In his world, tears were rare, the last resort of the desperate, and they were taken as seriously as a severe but temporary illness. His face was so shocked that Gareth was uncomfortable.

"What am I supposed to do about it if she cries?" he demanded.

"You could ask her why she's so sad," said James at once. "And . . . and . . ." He hesitated, remembering the things that were done in his own house during such crises. "Be nice! Make her a cup of tea. Or get chocolate."

Gareth snorted rudely and said, "As if!"

"That's not very nice," said James, which annoyed Gareth so much that he said threateningly, "Do you want me to carry this chicken or not?"

"Yes, yes, I do," said James, and scampered hurriedly round the corner and did not allow Gareth to catch up with him again until they reached the entrance to the old people's home.

"Round here!" he ordered then, heading for the little gate amongst the laurel bushes that led to the gardens. Two minutes later they were crouched by the raspberry canes, the mort had been retrieved, Gertie had been restored to her astonished companions, and James's mother was racing down the garden path, crying, "Boys! Boys! Boys!"

"I'm out of here," said Gareth, and ran, but James stood his ground as his mother flew to meet him.

"Hello, don't kiss me," he said.

Chapter Seventeen

It was dawn, but the little town was still asleep. The streets were empty until Gareth, on his way up the road to home, met Clem, on her way down. Clem looked less serene than her usual self. She pounced on Gareth the moment she saw him, demanding, "Tell me if you've seen Binny and James!" and as usual in her presence, Gareth found himself speechless.

"Don't just stand there staring at me!" snapped Clem. "Have you seen either of them? Answer! They've both disappeared!"

"I've only seen James," said Gareth, finding his voice.

"James! This morning? Where? I've looked and looked! His room is wrecked! When did you see him? Is he all right?"

"He's fine. He's with your mum. Down at the old people's place."

"Oh, thank goodness!" said Clem. "Oh, are you sure? With Mum? Did you see them together?"

"Yes. Outside, with those chickens . . ."

"Chickens," said Clem, and breathed with thankfulness, because after all she had imagined, chickens sounded so normal. "Chickens," she repeated, her whole face smooth with relief. "Oh, Gareth!" she said, and hugged him.

Gareth stood completely still, shocked. And then his shock was replaced by a wild, unusual desire to be the sort of person often hugged. Wanted. Useful.

"Binny might be down at the harbor," he suggested. "She goes there often. She does stupid things."

"What sort of stupid things?" demanded Clem sharply.

"You know, jump across the corner. Mess about on the wall." Gareth cast his mind back to remember the last thing he and Binny had dared each other to do. "Hang from that rail at the end."

"Hang . . ."

"By her knees," said Gareth helpfully, and then was not at all pleased that instead of being hugged for this useful information he was shoved roughly aside as Clem, looking absolutely horrified, began to run on down the road.

"Hey!" he called indignantly.

"What?" Clem stopped and spun round.

"You pushed me!"

"What? For goodness sake! Listen, if you see Binny, if

you meet her, tell her I'm looking for her. Say Clem's . . .
say Clem wasn't . . . it wasn't . . . say something! . . . Be nice!"

"Nice?" asked Gareth, but she had dismissed him and
was already far away.

Nice, thought Gareth, glaring and resentful. First James.
Now Clem. Telling him how to behave. Nicely.

His helpfulness vanished as if it had never been and was
replaced by a smoldering grumpiness. He marched home,
looking for trouble, avoided the front door, climbed the back
fence, and caught a glimpse of pink in the apple tree. Chaf-
finch? Flamingo? Binny.

Binny, with her seaweed hair all draggled with dew,
clutching a rose-splattered quilt and peering down at him.

"Hello," she said tentatively, not forgetting she was
dumped, and Gareth was instantly not nice.

"You look awful," he said. "What do you think you're
doing? That's such a pathetic place to hide."

"I'm not hiding," said Binny.

"Well, your sister's going mad looking for you. She thinks
you've jumped in the harbor or something. Have you been
sulking there all night?"

"I'm not sulking and I'm not hiding," said Binny. "I'm
just camping here because I want to."

"Oh yeah?" asked Gareth, smirking so much that she

added, "Our house is haunted, if you really want to know, and last night it was so awful I came out here instead."

"Haunted!" repeated Gareth derisively.

"I promise it's true," said Binny.

"Well, that's rubbish. If your house was haunted ours would be too. They're joined."

"I think," said Binny unhappily, but relieved in a way to say the words out loud, "it's . . . it's not so much the house that's haunted as me."

"Who'd haunt you?" asked Gareth contemptuously, and he was walking away when he heard the reply:

"Aunty Violet."

Gareth stopped dead.

"She's been haunting me all summer," said Binny, suddenly blurting out thoughts that had frightened her for weeks. "She used to watch me from that photograph. I could feel her eyes. And sometimes I see her. Just for a moment. Like in the street or through a window or something."

"Do you know how insane you sound?"

"Yes."

"And why would anyone bother to haunt anyone as boring as you?"

"Because of what I did."

"What was that, then? Murder her or something?"

His voice was so scornful that Binny said, "Yes," and began to cry.

Gareth stared up at her in surprise. Tears did not usually move him to any emotion except skepticism, but these tears looked real. He had never seen Binny cry before either. But murder? Binny? A girl who ushered flies out of windows and walked round ants?

"Really?" he asked, very interestedly. "How?"

"We had an awful fight. Awful. And I told her I wished she was dead. And she died."

"Right then?" asked Gareth, and his voice could not disguise the fact that he was seriously impressed.

"No, of course not right then!"

"What, like a few minutes after?"

"No."

"The same day, though?"

"I think it was about three weeks," said Binny, stiffly.

Gareth laughed so much he had to lean against the fence, and when he recovered he said, "So anyway, what was this ghost like that came and got you last night?"

"I don't want to talk about it."

"Go on, tell me what it looked like."

"It wasn't something I saw. It was something I heard. Noises."

"Go on!"

"Coffin noises," said Binny uncomfortably. "Like someone knocking to get out. Clawing and knocking. And rustlings and dragging sounds. Dead sounds. Like someone dead."

"So definitely not the sort of noises a chicken would make?" asked Gareth.

"What?"

"I mean, say some kid had stolen a chicken like, from an old people's home or something, and brought it home and hidden it in their bedroom till . . . Oh, your face! You should see it! Hidden it in their bedroom till they couldn't stand it any longer and then they thought it would be . . . would be . . ."—Gareth was having trouble speaking—"a good idea to stuff it . . ." He paused to howl, doubled up, rocking. "To stuff it in the attic!"

Binny stared, speechless.

"Definitely not that sort of noise, then?"

"OH!"

"Got it at last!"

Binny sat, stunned. Gareth gave himself up entirely to laughter. For Binny his hilarity was like cold water, or a hard white light. It washed away murk. It banished shadows. It freed her so completely from her fear of Aunty Violet that she scrambled down to the ground and stared around her, as if she had suddenly woken from a dream.

On Gareth's side of the fence a new voice called.

"Gareth! Gareth!"

"Her," Binny heard Gareth breathe.

"Gareth, we've been so worried! Oh, please don't walk away! We didn't know what to think! Your room empty, and the front door wide open. Your father is out looking for you. Where on earth have you been?"

"Mind your own," said Gareth.

His laughter was over, and his voice was so insolent that Binny shivered, as if a shadow had blotted out the sun. She was glad she was out of sight on the other side of the fence. A moment later she was even more thankful because Gareth's father had clearly overheard Gareth's latest remark. Binny recognized his thunderous, furious, end-of-patience roar.

"GARETH! GO TO YOUR ROOM!"

Binny heard Gareth give a bleat of defiance.

"AT ONCE!"

Another bleat. Shaken but indignant.

"AND STAY THERE!"

Then nothing more until a great slam.

That was the door.

★   ★   ★

Binny's own home was not tranquil either. The first person she met was Clem, carefully stirring a mug of coffee and unable to meet her eyes.

"Bin. Binny."

"Oh, hello," said Binny, uncertainly, and stood hovering on one foot.

"You came down last night."

"It's all right," said Binny.

"No, it isn't."

"I won't tell. And anyway, you had your clothes on and everything. Most of them. I saw."

"Binny!" wailed Clem.

"Do you think . . ." asked Binny, her voice wobbling a little (*Oh, Liam, oh, Clem, oh,* Sweet Belinda, *the boat that never sailed*), "do you think I can still be crew?"

"Of course you can! Why shouldn't you? Forever, if you want!"

"Well, then there's no need to look so bothered. It wasn't awful. You weren't snoring or dribbling or anything like that."

"Binny, did you stand and stare?"

"Yes."

"And then went back to bed?"

"No. I went outside. To the apple tree. I always wanted to

try sleeping in the apple tree . . . Hello, James! Hello, Mum!"

There they were, one jubilant, one rather weary.

"Guess what?" cried James, forgetting even his usual greeting, and thrust forward his chest so that Binny could read a cardboard badge pinned with a large safety pin to the front of his wetsuit.

JAMES CORNWALLIS
CHIEF CHICKEN KEEPER

"That's me! I get paid too! A pound a week and I've got to count the chickens every day and tell someone if any go missing! And see here! Two things!"

He held out his fat closed fists.

"One egg! For me!" He uncurled the fingers of his left hand. "Nobody else to eat it! AND!" With a flourish he opened his right. "One ruby! Red! Look!"

He held out his palm to show a glowing crimson marvel, perhaps not a ruby, but something just as red. "From my mort! To keep forever. I gave the rest back! I was very, very good."

"I don't know about that," said his mother.

"And I've worked out what to do next. I'm having ducks and I'm digging a lake . . ."

"Pond," corrected his mother from the background.

"There'll be a railway track all around," continued the undaunted duck farmer. "And Binny, you were MAD to tell me to keep that chicken in my bedroom! You should see the mess it made! I had to put it in the attic and I've been awake nearly all night!"

"So have I," said Binny. "I had to go and sleep in the apple tree because of your awful chicken, which I did NOT tell you—"

"You spent the night in the apple tree?" demanded her mother. "James spent the night chasing chickens around the roof! You spent the night in the apple tree. Clem, please tell me you at least were respectably asleep in bed!"

Clem's eyes met Binny's.

"Clem?" asked their mother. "Clem?"

"Come on, James, I'll cook your egg for you," said Binny, and led the way into the kitchen and discreetly closed the door.

The house became very quiet. The door to the living room remained closed. James fell asleep before his egg could be eaten, pillowed at the table upon a slice of buttered toast. Binny left him there and crept upstairs. Her bedroom felt empty. Unhaunted. She had the strangest feeling of loss.

"Aunty Violet," she said, testing the words aloud, the way she would have prodded a bruise to see if it still hurt.

The words fell cool as sea foam and left no echo in the air.

Binny's thoughts were all bewildered.

Did I stop hating Aunty Violet?

Does that mean I don't love Max?

Out loud she said his name, "Max," and felt the familiar hurt of memory, and was glad it was still there.

I'll write more letters, Binny vowed. I'll get more addresses. I'll find more people to ask. I'll . . .

But somehow, it seemed hopeless.

Binny shook herself crossly and pushed open her window to catch her glimpse of sea.

Voices.

Gareth and his father.

I shouldn't listen, thought Binny, but she did.

"We came back to this place to please you. That was the only reason. You know that. *Don't* shrug!"

"Get the moaning over with, then," said Gareth.

"You've turned this whole summer into a battle."

"Yes, I have. I meant to."

"You've said over and over, from the first day, that you want to leave."

"So?"

"So, all right. You win. You can go."

"What?"

"That's what you wanted, isn't it? I'll drive you back to your mother's this afternoon. Start packing."

There was such a long silence that Binny thought that perhaps Gareth's father had left the room and Gareth was alone again. Then she heard him speak.

"So she stays and I go?"

"That's the way things seem to be at the moment."

"What about she goes and I stay?"

"Not an option."

"How long is this going to last?" burst out Gareth. "You and Her? It's gone on for ages! How long more?"

"I hope for a very long time," replied his father. "I hope we'll be married for a very long time."

Gareth's father really did leave then. Binny heard Gareth's bedroom door open and close. She heard furious slamming as Gareth flung his possessions about. She heard a miserable sniffing and she waited tactfully until it was over before putting her head out of the window and calling, "Gareth! Gareth!"

"Clear off!"

"I heard."

"I don't care if you did."

"Didn't you know they were going to get married until just now?"

"Think they tell me anything?"

"I'm sorry you're going. I wish you weren't."

Kindness from an enemy was too much for Gareth. He disappeared back inside his room very abruptly and remained there while Binny listened to the nasty sounds of tears and a runny nose being dealt with without a hand-kerchief.

Then his head appeared again.

"Say bye to James for me."

"I will. Wait! Wait, Gareth! About your bike. I'll save up. As soon as I can. I promise I will."

Gareth gave a bit of a laugh, a proper one, not a snigger. "You needn't worry. It was insured."

"It was what?"

"Insured."

"What does that mean?"

"It means you needn't worry."

He sounded utterly forlorn.

Binny racked her brains for something useful she could say. "Perhaps when you get used to the idea, you won't mind so much. She was nice to me when Cinders got into your house."

"I waited and waited for this summer!" exploded Gareth, all at once. "All those useless vacations I got dragged off on! Rotten France! Stupid California! And then I finally got him to come back here and he went and brought her too! And now the whole summer's been wasted!"

"Not all of it," said Binny. "You liked . . . you liked . . ." she hesitated—"James, and his poisonous lettuce. That day when we saw the adder . . . the little adder . . ." Binny was making an enormous attempt to reach Gareth in his unhappy, distant world. "When we went on your bike all the way to the rock pools. Those times weren't wasted."

"I wish we'd got that net," said Gareth bitterly. "I'd have gone last week if I hadn't hurt my arm again. I bet that Liam never bothered."

Binny was sure he was right, but at the same time she was suddenly pleased. Something real she could do, to cheer Gareth up.

"I'll go and see," she said. "If it's still there, I'll get it."

"You never could. From that boat? He wouldn't let you."

"Not from the boat, from the shore. Out by the cliff path, the way we did before."

"That net's much farther out than those rock pools."

"So?"

"And I bet it's heavy. You could never manage. It would take both of us . . ."

Gareth paused. Gazed at Binny. Flexed his shoulder where the sling had been.

"Bin! Let's go! Come on!"

He was transformed. Glasses glinting. All alive.

"But how can we? Your father! And I heard, you're supposed to be packing! And anyway, your arm!"

"It's better. Much better than it was. Quick, while we can get away, before my dad comes back."

"He'll be furious."

"Who cares? It'll be fun. Come on, Bin!"

"Do you mean right now?"

"There only is now."

Still Binny hesitated.

"Dare you!"

"All right. I suppose. All right."

That was how Gareth and Binny came to travel to the point where a blue net was tangled on a rock, and the lichens were black and green and gold, and at certain times and tides the seals gathered and Liam begrudgingly tracked them down to please his cargo of holidaymakers.

★   ★   ★

It took a long time to reach the point. By the time Binny and Gareth arrived, they were like people who had traveled beyond the usual pattern of time. The events that had led them there were far in the past. The future was a vagueness just below the horizon.

Until the tide came in.

Then, there they were, trapped. With their missing glasses, dodgy arms, dropped-in-a-rock-pool cell phone, and inadequate swimming skills.

Although not without hope.

There was the hope that their rocky headland might not totally submerge. There was the thought that even if it did, it would only be for a while, and by hanging on to the net and each other, they might make it through the high tide, wet but alive.

"Of course, it depends how deep the water gets over the rocks," said Binny, whose idea this had been. "I mean knee-deep or head-deep."

"I know what you *mean*," said Gareth impatiently.

As well as these hopes, there was the one that the soaked cell phone (still locked on a screen that would not change) might dry out in time for them to call for help.

Last of all, there was the hope of the seals.

The seals were still with them. The tide that had so ferociously driven Binny and Gareth until they were marooned on their island had hardly disturbed the seals at all. The ones on the rocks moved higher for their sunbathing. The ones in the sea appeared and disappeared, hunting dabs and mackerel. Once Binny saw one come up with a fish. It flipped it round lengthways and swallowed it whole.

"I'm not really hungry," said Binny. "Are you?"

"I'm all right."

Away at the harbor Liam would be loading his boat with holidaymakers. Binny could picture him, promising seals and photo opportunities, making the most of the warmth after the week of rain. Eventually, if the seals stayed, he would come and find them.

"All we have to do is wait," said Binny, and Gareth refrained from pointing out that all they really could do was wait, and instead said, "I told you my worst thing that happened to me. When my parents split. So what was yours?"

Chapter Eighteen

To pass the wait with talking did not seem unreasonable. Better than panicking, and anyway, if the tide really did come in as far as Binny hoped it wouldn't, and Gareth was certain it would, they had better get their talking done now. In case there was no later.

"The worst thing that ever happened to me," said Binny, "was when my father died."

Gareth nodded sympathetically.

"I suppose," added Binny.

"What do you mean? *You suppose?*"

"I know it *was* the worst," said Binny, sprawled like a washed-up mermaid on their diminishing outcrop of rock. "It just doesn't *feel* the worst. Like when I broke my elbow when I was little. I broke my elbow, and then only a few days later I shut my fingers in the car door. My elbow *was* the worst, but my fingers *felt* worse."

"So what feels worst?"

"Losing my dog," said Binny so promptly that Gareth flinched. "Losing my dog and people saying things like, 'Well, Binny, you'll understand one day that it was probably for the best.' Nobody said it was probably for the best when Dad died."

"But your dog didn't die," said Gareth, and then became very red and wished he had not spoken, because how could he know that?

"He might have," said Binny, not noticing Gareth's blushes. "Anything might have happened to him. I don't know."

Gareth knew. Ever since Binny had lost his bike, he had known. He had tried to push the knowledge away—and then push Binny away . . . but they both had stayed.

"All this fuss about a dog," continued Binny. "That's what people said. They couldn't understand."

Gareth could understand. *All this fuss about a dog.* He had been hearing it himself all summer.

"So what was he like, your dog?" he asked, fiddling with his useless iPhone, putting off the moment when he would have to admit what he knew.

Binny's face became suddenly bright.

"Oh," she said. "Well, he was perfect. Black and white. A border collie. A border collie puppy, really, just like the picture in a book I had once. He was eight weeks old when I was eight years old. I got him on my birthday. He was the only thing I wanted. The only thing I asked for. Him, and nothing else."

"Um," said Gareth, with begrudging understanding. How well he knew the power of demanding *one thing and nothing else*. No fallback. No compromise. No escape route for the present buyers that did not include a shuffling, guilty shame.

"Mum said," continued Binny, her eyes on the boat-less horizon but sticking resolutely to the undrowned past, "'Not a puppy! Especially not a border collie puppy. They need hours and hours of exercise! Think of something else!' But I didn't."

Binny paused, not elaborating on how completely she hadn't. How she took the border collie book to bed with her, open at the page with the picture of the puppy. How sometimes during the day she would look wistfully at a patch of puppy-shaped space and say, "I wish . . ." very quietly.

"And on my birthday, there he was," said Binny, "the best surprise ever! And Mum said, 'Oh no! Oh no! That's why you spent half the night in the garage!' and Dad said, 'I thought we could manage, between us, and with this enormous garden.' And we did. Only then everything went wrong."

Gareth became very involved in trying to pry an

enormous limpet from a rock. The limpet, who had resided comfortably in that spot for more years than Gareth had been alive, refused to have anything to do with his plans. Binny, having lingered so happily over the good part of her story, the picture book puppy, the perfect surprise, hurried quickly through the rest: her father's death, bankruptcy, moving out of the family home, Granny, the terrible problem of a large, bouncy border collie and a very old lady sharing a house. Then Aunty Violet, the loss of Max, and her quest ever since to discover what happened to him. Ending with the letters.

"Couldn't you just get another dog?"

"Another?" asked Binny, and she sounded as shocked as if Gareth had asked, "Couldn't you just get another father?"

"I suppose it wouldn't be the same," admitted Gareth, and then he made up his mind at last. The frozen image was still locked on the screen of his phone.

He passed it to Binny.

At first she did not understand. She asked, "What?" and looked uncomprehendingly at the picture of a sturdy black and white collie dog grinning at the photographer.

"That's Max." Gareth spoke as huskily as James had when he said, "That's my mort," but Binny replied quite matter-of-factly, "No, it isn't. He wasn't that sort of collie. Much thinner, and his fur was quite short. A bit tufty, but not all feathers. Who is that dog?"

"It's Max. I took it just before I came away."

"You took it?"

"In our garden. In Oxford."

"How could . . . ?" Binny paused, and looked at the picture again. Those eyes . . . that laughing, tongue-lolling grin . . . "How could it be Max? You took it? Is it a dog you know, then? Is it another dog called Max that you think might be my Max?"

"Listen," said Gareth a bit desperately. "I told you about the last summer we were here. Two years ago. Mum and Dad, and the fights, and how I used to get over your fence and hide in your garden. I made a den, I called it my camp. No one knew. Everywhere was all overgrown like it was when you came, and the cottage was empty. Vacation people hardly ever stayed there, because it was such a mess. Then one day there was a dog in the garden, and it was Max."

"How?" demanded Binny, fiercely. "How?"

"Miss Cornwallis that you call Aunty Violet turned up with him."

Binny's mouth fell open.

"He was all on his own out there, whining. He had water and food, and stuff, but he wanted someone to play with."

"Did you play with him?" asked Binny in a small, lost voice.

"For hours. He chased a red rubber ring, and hid in the long grass and rolled and jumped and flopped down and chewed my sneakers. It was the best day for ages. Forever, actually. And then it seemed to go quiet and I looked up and there was everyone watching me over the fence. And smiling and smiling. Mum and Dad and Miss Cornwallis. She must have gone round to ours. And Dad said, 'Gareth, he's yours if you want him.'"

"YOURS!"

"And Mum and Miss Cornwallis nodded."

Tears were rolling down Binny's cheeks, floods, from her shining, astonished eyes. She said, "Max is all right? He didn't go to kennels, or a rescue home? He's been safe with you all this time?"

"Yes. With me and Mum in school time, and me and Dad in the vacations."

"But where is he now?"

"With Mum. Because I couldn't bring him. Because of Her."

"She's allergic," murmured Binny.

Gareth looked at her for the first time since he had begun his story. He saw how she stared at the tiny picture frozen on the screen. He saw how tightly she held it.

"Sometimes I even thought he might be dead."

"I took him to puppy training. He's learned to do all sorts."

"I always knew he was clever."

"He understands everything. Every word. He can tell the time. He can guess your thoughts. He gets jokes. He's the only dog I've ever seen that laughs."

"I know. I remember."

"I don't know what he thought when I left him behind in Oxford. This summer has just got worse and worse. Leaving Max. Her. Dad wouldn't get rid of Her, whatever I did. And he wouldn't give in and send me back to Mum. And then I found out about you, and that Max had been yours. I was scared stiff you'd come round and Dad would get to know. He thought Miss Cornwallis had got Max from an old lady who couldn't manage him anymore. I suppose she did. Your granny. Dad never guessed about any other family, though. Neither did Mum."

"Did you?"

Gareth glanced round. A blurry horizon. Water. Rock. Binny. No escape.

"I always thought he wasn't really like an old lady's dog. He knew so many games. And then, last winter, a letter came. From Miss Cornwallis. From Spain."

"WHAT!"

As well as he could, Gareth recalled the letter that had made his spine prickle with fear. Forwarded by the cleaner from the seaside house to his mother's home. *To Whom It May Concern (re: the dog Max)*. Found by Gareth himself on the doormat amongst all the other mail. Grabbed, ripped open, hidden, destroyed, but never forgotten.

I have recently learned that the original family are anxious to trace . . .

Should you ever wish to part . . .

Assurances of his health and well-being would be very gratefully received . . .

All beautifully typed and signed, on behalf of Miss Violet Cornwallis.

And underneath, in a terrible scrawl, *I should have asked long ago.*

"Aunty Violet," whispered Binny.

"Yes," said Gareth. "I know I should have told you before. He's your dog. Your dad gave him to you."

"Yes, he did," agreed Binny. "Yes. Isn't it strange? Your dad gave him to you. My dad gave him to me."

"I wish it hadn't happened that way. I'm sorry your dad died."

Binny gazed out to sea.

"He couldn't help it," she said.

It was the first time she had ever admitted that truth. Her father had died, but he hadn't meant to. He hadn't meant any of it. All the consequences that had come afterward, right down to their perilous position on this rock, had followed as inevitably as the rising of the tide.

"Are the seals still all there?" asked Gareth, sensibly changing the subject.

"They have to be," said Binny, "so that Liam will come and look for them. I wish we had some fish. They'd stay for fish. Do they just eat fish, Gareth? What about seaweed?"

"No," said Gareth, and as if in agreement a seal slipped into the water.

"Limpets?"

"Don't think so."

Another seal left the rocks to swim, half-upright, watching for the rest of the group.

"I was really angry with Dad when he died. The way he just vanished. One day there, playing trains with James, listening to Clem's flute. Then. Gone. No more anything. No more..."

Binny paused.

"Stories."

Games for James. Music for Clem. And stories for herself. Amazement and relief swept over Binny like waves. There were three seals in the water now, and the others were looking restless, but Binny's unreliable heart took off like a seagull and went soaring into the sky.

"I forgot!" she said. "Stories!"

It was as if she heard her father's voice again. *A long, long time ago, in the days when there were heroes.*

"Gareth! Can you sing?"

"What!"

"Sing! To the seals! They like singing. I remember it from one of Dad's stories! There was a girl, and she sang on the seashore, and the seals came to listen!"

"You can't believe that!"

"Daddy did."

"It was just a story, though, Bin," said Gareth.

"Yes, but stories are important. My father said they were. He said sometimes stories can save your life. There's another seal gone! Come on, Gareth!"

"I don't think . . ." began Gareth, but Binny was already off. The first song that came into her head.

"The holly and the ivy . . ."

"But that's a Christmas carol!" protested Gareth.

"Doesn't matter! *When they are both full grown . . .* Look! That seal's listening! *Of all the trees that are in the wood . . .* There's another looking too! Definitely! *The holly bears the crown!"*

Gareth, in his short-sighted world, could not tell whether the seals were listening or not. Without his glasses all he could see were heavy gray shapes on the rocks. Still, perhaps . . . Worth a try.

"Please, Gareth!"

Might as well.

Gareth's voice, choir trained, clear as Clem's flute, rose suddenly beside Binny.

"I wore my coat (we did *Joseph* at school)

With golden lining (I was Joseph)

Bright colors shining . . ."

The faraway seal had vanished, but now he reappeared, directly beneath them, his face turned toward Gareth.

"Wonderful and new."

"He's pleased!" whispered Binny. "His face is smiling!"

"And in the east," continued Gareth, shaking his head disapprovingly at the idea that a seal would smile, *"The dawn was breaking . . ."*

Max, thought Binny, I've found Max!

"And the world was waking . . ."

We can share!

"Any dream will do."

Joseph ended, and Binny began "Lavender's Blue," and that led them into nursery rhymes, and soon there was no doubt that Binny's father's story had been correct. They had an audience down there by the water. Seven seals.

A song about frogs. "Johnny Appleseed," and then, just as Gareth was proving that he knew all the words of "American Pie," Binny leaped to her feet.

"Liam! Liam!"

"I can't see anything."

"It is! I promise!" Binny began bouncing up and down, calling, waving.

"Bin! Sit down! You'll scare them!"

"It doesn't matter now. Liam's seen us. They're waving! Gareth! Gareth! It's going to be all right! Everything's going to be all right!"

"Is it? What'll Liam say? What am I going to do about my Dad and Her? What's going to happen to Max?"

"Liam won't mind! We're a photo opportunity! You'll just have to make friends with your dad and her. Max couldn't be easier. We can share! You in the school times.

Me in the vacations when you're staying with your dad."

Gareth looked up in amazement.

"Could we really?"

"Why not? We've shared things all summer."

Gareth began to grin.

The seal boat was so close now that even he could see it. Voices called to them, shrieking with concern.

"He's got two life preservers. One each. Perfect. Turn your back to the wind, though, if you think you're going to be sick. There's one seal left. Let's sing to it!"

"You're a bit mad, Bin, you know that?"

"Do you think Max will have forgotten me?"

Gareth looked at her. Soaked. Bedraggled. Arms full of fishing net. Bouncing with excitement on the top of a rock. Singing, *"DON'T stop me now! I'm having a good time!"* Sending the last seal diving to the depths. He didn't think Max would have forgotten her. He didn't think anyone ever could. He said, trying to sound casual, "Oh, I shouldn't think so. No. Probably not."

At home, the escape of Gareth, and the absence of Binny had not gone unnoticed.

"Off with that girl!" growled Gareth's father.

"Off with that boy," said Clem.

Time went on, and the worrying began.

"It's not like Binny..."

"It's just like Gareth."

"He'll be all right," said James comfortingly to Gareth's father when he came round hoping for news. "I haven't given him any lettuce for ages. He isn't poisoned anyway."

"Poisoned?" asked Gareth's bewildered father.

"It's just a game," said Binny's mother soothingly. "You do keep trying his phone?"

"It appears to have gone dead," said Gareth's father.

Dead was a disturbing word, even when it was just about phones. They began searching places. The beaches, the harbor, the library, Kate's.

Kate privately called Liam.

"Not seen a sight of them," he told her. "They'll have done something silly."

Kate reported the first half of the message, but not the second.

"You'll see I'm right," said Liam, although his first words when he saw them were, "I don't believe it!"

"I don't believe it! I don't believe it! I don't believe it!" said Liam, at his first glimpse of Binny waving from her rock, and he pulled out his phone and called Kate.

"Both of them!" he told her. "I might have known, I might have known, I might have known!"

He kept repeating these words as he passed over life jackets, threw them the life preservers, and stowed them on board, first Binny, then Gareth.

"And the net!" said Binny triumphantly. "Liam, does the tide come over those rocks?"

"Would you like to wait a bit and find out?"

"Not really," said Binny, so they headed back to the harbor, where there was quite a crowd gathered to welcome the boat.

Kate exclaimed, "What a crew!"

"Kate!" cried Binny. "Something wonderful!"

Binny's mother said, "Binny, Bin, Belinda!" having not yet recovered from the shock of the phone call that had summoned her there.

"Mum, the best news in the world!"

"Hello! Don't kiss me!"

"James! You'll never guess!"

Clem said nothing at all, but she clutched Binny tight, as if she might disappear back in the sea, and Binny clutched her back and said, "Clem, Clem, Clem."

"What?"

"I've found Max!"

Gareth didn't say anything, but he allowed himself to be hugged, both by his father and Her. He had distracted himself from seasickness by preparing a speech of apology, but it was not needed. All that he had to do to be forgiven, it seemed, was to come back undrowned.

Instead of driving Gareth to Oxford that evening, Gareth's father drove there alone. And he returned, not alone, very early in the morning.

Max came rollicking into Binny's bedroom at dawn that day, and from the moment he saw her it was perfectly obvious that he had never forgotten her. He flung himself upon her, whimpering with joy.

"Max!" cried Binny, lost as usual between laughter and tears.

There was never any doubt that Max was the most intelligent dog in the world. Vacations with Binny, school time with Gareth caused him no confusion at all. He was admired by everyone. Over the fence, by Gareth's father's new wife.

With caution by Cinderella. Disbelievingly by James, who nearly fell over with shock when Max, instead of chewing his legs, kindly offered a paw to be shaken.

Gareth and Binny glowed with pride at each new conquest. However, the person who regarded Max with the greatest pleasure of all was Aunty Violet, age sixteen, retrieved from the restaurant wall. There she was, in Binny's bedroom, looking as pleased as if she had planned the whole astonishing affair, and Binny thought, *If.*

If it hadn't snowed, and Clem hadn't fainted, and Aunty Violet and I had never been stuck in that car together, she would never have known how much I missed Max. She would never have sent me her particular regards or left us her house. James wouldn't have started a farm, nor collected a mort, nor swapped it for a chicken. There would never have been a chicken in the attic to scare me, and so I would never have gone down to look for Clem. I wouldn't have found her with Liam. I would never have slept in the apple tree because I wouldn't have run away. Gareth wouldn't have had to help take the chicken back to the old ladies, and he wouldn't have come home and found me there. She wouldn't have come running when she saw us talking, and Gareth wouldn't have said to her, "Mind your own." Then his father wouldn't have got furious and sent him upstairs and I wouldn't have found out he was being sent home.

Gareth would have gone to find the fishing net on his own.

And he'd have spent too long staring in rock pools and losing his glasses and getting fish hooks in his arm. He'd have got stuck, just the same, but without me.

And I'd never have known what happened to Max. I think the seals would have swum away. And Liam told me afterward that the sea does come over those rocks. I think Gareth would have drowned.

He didn't know the story.

Sometimes stories can save your life. Dad told me so many. I'm going to write them down.

A long, long time ago, in the days when there were heroes, which there still are, and nearly all girls too, there was a little house, in a little town, right on the edge of a wild, rocky coast. Right on the edge of the land this town was built, houses spilling down to the rocks. Salt spray blowing up the streets. Rock and stone and salt and wind and a sort of lightness in the air.

And in that town there lived a girl.

Call her Binny . . .